Allan Warren

I0557042

THE SWEET REVENGE OF PETER BROCK

by

Allan Warren

BUNNYWAR BOOKS

To Lipsy

The Sweet Revenge of Peter Brock

First published in 2024
by Bunnywar Books, London

Disclaimer:

The young CECIL O'DOCHERTY
Charming, handsome, rough, in his late twenties.

PEGGY O'BRIAN
Fading good looks, brassy. In her mid to late thirties.

PETER BROCK
Goodlooking, bright. In his early twenties.

PETER BROCK alias CECIL O'DOCHERTY
Charming and handsome. In his mid seventies.

EDITH
A faded beauty, stylish. In her early to mid sixties.

DAME SYBIL
Grand, elegant, formidable. In her early to mid seventies.

SIR JOHN CHARLESGUD
Ruddy-faced, pompous. In his mid seventies.

YOUNG SIR JOHN CHARLESGUD
Handsome, arrogant. in his thirties.

ROY DEAN
Handsome, stylish. In his late seventies.

OLDER PEGGY O'BRIAN
Frail, in her mid to late seventies.

DOCTOR GRIMSHAW
Average looking. In his fifties.

The Sweet Revenge of Peter Brock

A SUMMER'S AFTERNOON - PRESENT DAY - 1985

THE LOUNGE OF DANTON MANOR. A RETIREMENT HOME FOR THEATRICALS IN A SUBURB OF LONDON. THE ROOM IS SPACIOUS AND PLEASANTLY DECORATED. STAGE RIGHT IS THE ENTRANCE. UPSTAGE CENTRE IS A BAR WHERE SOME OF THE RESIDENTS ARE HAVING A DRINK. OTHERS ARE PLAYING CARDS OR CHATTING.

Peter Brock alias Cecil O'Docherty, is leaning against the bar, sipping champagne, while laughing and joking with other retired actors who are hanging on his every word. He's stylishly dressed, sporting a polka dot cravat and blazer. On the other side of the lounge, two elegant elderly actresses are sipping sherry and chatting as they look over in Peter's direction.

EDITH
You've got to hand it to him.

DAME SYBIL
Who dear?

EDITH
Our Mr Brock. He's only been here three months and already has them eating out of his hand.

DAME SYBIL
More like drinking out of it, you mean.

EDITH
Perhaps, but you must admit he is very popular.

DAME SYBIL
So would you be if you constantly bought drinks for everybody.

EDITH
Not everyone. We buy or own, remember?

DAME SYBIL
And so does Roy Dean. *(DAME SYBIL looks over at ROY DEAN, who is at another table, watching all the comings and goings. Although in his late seventies, Roy is still very handsome and also very smartly dressed)* Funny, how he sits over there, glowering at Mr Brock, or whatever his name is. I don't think he likes him.

EDITH
I adore him. I should make more of an effort to talk to him.

DAME SYBIL
Then do. That is, if you can fight your way through the scrum. Who knows, he might even buy you a drink.

EDITH
No, not him. I meant Roy Dean.

DAME SYBIL
Well, good luck with that one. He enjoys his privacy too much.

EDITH
I don't blame him. He must be knocking on a bit by now.

DAME SYBIL
I'd hate to be the one to shatter your delusion, but we're not exactly in the first flush of youth ourselves.

EDITH
I remember seeing him in films when he was a matinee idol.

DAME SYBIL
That's going back a bit.

EDITH
No wonder he keeps himself to himself. He must have had his fair share of stupid young girls fawning over him.

DAME SYBIL
Then, console yourself. At least you only fit into one of those categories.

EDITH
(Dame SYBIL Ignores EDITH'S remark) How does he do it? I wonder.

DAME SYBIL
Easy, he sits there and ignores people.

EDITH
I meant Mr Brock.

DAME SYBIL
(DAME SYBIL gestures toward CECIL) Oh, him. How does he do what?

EDITH
Pay for it all. It's not as if it's just a one-off.

DAME SYBIL
I know, dear. He does it every time he's in here.

EDITH
And to think. We can barely afford to buy our own. Let alone free drinks for that lot. Just look at them. It's pathetic.

DAME SYBIL
It's regrettable to see Sir Jonathan Charlesgud joining in. Who would have thought? The finest Shakespearean actor of his generation could be bought for the price of whiskey and soda. My god, he was so handsome when he was younger.

EDITH
He's not bad now. If he were ever sober, I'd still give him ago.

DAME SYBIL
You wouldn't? Anyway, you couldn't.

EDITH
Get over it. I'm still pretty limber.

DAME SYBIL
I can't even remember when I last went out on a date.

EDITH
I do. He took me on a day trip to Brighton.

DAME SYBIL
Don't tell me. It was raining.

EDITH
No, sunny as anything. We even had a stroll on the beach.

DAME SYBIL
So what was the problem?

EDITH
It was when he complimented me on my snakeskin shoes.

DAME SYBIL
You should be grateful for a compliment at your age.

EDITH
I would have been, but I wasn't wearing any shoes!

DAME SYBIL
You silly thing. *(they both giggle)*

EDITH
They do say when there's still a fire below. You need someone with a very large hose to put it out.

DAME SYBIL
You can be so vulgar at times.

EDITH
Vulgar? Why? What did I say?

DAME SYBIL
It's not what you said. It's what you meant.

EDITH
At our age, it's too late to be prudish dear.

DAME SYBIL
Can you believe it, I'll be sixty-eight next month.

EDITH
Easily. But what's age got to do with anything? I intend to try and fit in a few last flings by the time I get to your age.

DAME SYBIL
But I'm only two years older than you.

EDITH
Not mentally, dear. Granted, seventy is not exactly young. But you behave like you're ready to be wrapped in bandages and exhibited in the basement of the British Museum.

DAME SYBIL
And you behave as if you're still a spring chicken. It's time you faced up to reality.

EDITH
What would either of us know about reality? We're just a couple of aged actors who sold fantasy for a living.

DAME SYBIL
Yes, I suppose we are. D'you know. I still get fan mail addressed to Princess Anastasia and Jehanne D'Arc from when I played Joan of Arc.

EDITH
I hate to remind you. But it won't be too long before you'll have to go through that whole cremation scene all over again. The only diffrence, next time, it'll be for real.

DAME SYBIL
(DAME SYBIL looks to the heavens) Your idea of humour never changes.

EDITH
(Edith looks around) Unlike our surroundings.

DAME SYBIL
You must miss your lovely home. Imagine what a house in Mayfair is worth now.

EDITH
I dread to think. If only my husband had made better investments before he died. I wouldn't have had to sell it and end up penniless in this dump.

DAME SYBIL
It's hardly a dump.

EDITH
Well, it's not exactly a five-star hotel.

DAME SYBIL
Just be grateful. After all, we are heavily subsidised.

EDITH
Admittedly, it's far more comfortable than the average care home. And at least we have something in common with the other residents.

DAME SYBIL
(She looks over at the bar, where some residents are getting loud) Hopefully, you didn't mean that in the literal sense. Whoever dragged them out of the chorus has a lot to answer for.

EDITH
Don't be such a snob. You seem to forget. We were also in the chorus, remember?

DAME SYBIL
But that was such a long time ago it's easy to slip one's mind.

EDITH
And we would have stayed there if we hadn't married well.

DAME SYBIL
Do you miss him?

EDITH
Who dear?

DAME SYBIL
Your husband.

EDITH
No, why would I? He was terrible sex.

DAME SYBIL
Oh, Edith!

EDITH
Well, it's true. In the end, the only thing we had in common was being married on the same day.

DAME SYBIL
I was lucky. As you know, I loved my husband, and he left me well provided for. It was me who frittered it all away. So be grateful you haven't yourself to blame.

EDITH
Maybe, but at least you had fun doing it.

DAME SYBIL
True! But I do miss Denham.

EDITH
Denim? No, dear, stick to your twinset and fake pearls. They suit you much better.

DAME SYBIL
I meant my house in Denham.

EDITH
Yes, we did have some wonderful times there. Georgian, wasn't it?

DAME SYBIL
Some parts date back to Cromwell's time.

EDITH
I remember that weekend you had Noël Coward stay. You couldn't have wished for a better house guest.

DAME SYBIL
Yes, Noël was so much fun. Sadly, like so many. He's no longer with us anymore.

EDITH
He was always so witty and amusing. What was that song he kept playing? You know, the one about somebody's daughter.

DAME SYBIL
You mean. Don't put your daughter on the stage Mrs Worthington.

EDITH
Yes, that was it. *(EDITH starts to sing)* Don't put your daughter on the stage Mrs...

DAME SYBIL
(DAME SYBIL joins in) Worthington.
Don't put your daughter on the stage.
She's a bit of an ugly duckling
You must honestly confess
And the width of her seat
Would surely defeat
Any chances of success!
(They giggle, then notice the other residents looking in their direction, including CECIL)

EDITH
Oh dear, Mr Brock is looking over.

DAME SYBIL
Then look away.

EDITH
I wonder where he got all that money to splash about so freely.

DAME SYBIL
No idea.

EDITH
I never worked with him, did you?

DAME SYBIL
I can't recall doing so. But then, who knows perhaps, I did. But you know what my memory is like.

EDITH
(to herself) Usually very convenient.

DAME SYBIL
If it serves me correctly.

EDITH
I'll be a first if it does.

DAME SYBIL
I think I've seen him in something. It might have been one of those low-budget films.

EDITH
He probably played small parts with very few lines.

DAME SYBIL
So, where did he get his money?

EDITH
Inheritance? Maybe, unlike us, he saved his.

DAME SYBIL
But at least we had fun spending it. Just think of the parties we gave. I remember the shock on your face when I turned up with Edward VIII on my arm. You didn't look pleased. I think you were jealous.

EDITH
Oh, be fair. I didn't have time to be. Edward discarded you at the front door as quickly as his overcoat.

DAME SYBIL
Absolute nonsense!

EDITH
Be honest. You know he did. The moment he saw that dreadful Mrs Simpson draped over the piano singing along to Cole Porter. Do you remember that awful dress she wore exposing her skinny back?

DAME SYBIL
How could I forget? It went all the way down to her bony bum. I didn't stand a chance after that. So, it's thanks to you. I'm now sitting here rather than at Buckingham Palace!

EDITH
Not really, dear. Future Kings don't marry actresses.

DAME SYBIL
(DAME SYBIL gestures toward CECIL) It's sad to think if only we had done the same as our mystery man over there.

EDITH
Meaning?

DAME SYBIL
Tucked something away for the future. Then we wouldn't be sitting here nursing a sticky sherry, Instead of a nice bottle of bubbly.

EDITH
Then thank god for small mercies. You know what happens when you drink champagne.

DAME SYBIL
If you're insinuating, it goes straight to my head. It's not true.

EDITH
It wasn't your head I was thinking of. Quite the reverse.

DAME SYBIL
What are you implying?

EDITH
Oh, come off it. When you drink champagne, it's like sitting next to a volcano. *(EDITH chuckles)* You know it gives you the most terrible wind.

DAME SYBIL
Absolute nonsense!

EDITH
(CECIL looks over in their direction and smiles) Give him one of your 'hello, but don't come over' waves.

DAME SYBIL
Do you mean when I wave, smile and then immediately turn away?

EDITH
Yes, the one you do when you don't want someone joining your table. It works wonders.

DAME SYBIL
(DAME SYBIL does it) Oh. It didn't work. *(at that moment, the waiter comes with a tray with two large glasses of champagne and takes away their empty sherry glasses)*

EDITH
Indeed. Well, if you are going to drink that. I'd best prepare myself. *(EDITH hands her a cushion. Then dips into her bag and sprays some cologne on herself and then a couple of squirts in the air).*

DAME SYBIL
You are too awful. *(as EDITH and DAME SYBIL look over at CEC-IL, he raises his glass and toasts them. DAME SYBIL and EDITH look at the large glasses of champagne and nervously smile. Then, slowly pick them up. DAME SYBIL winks at EDITH)* Oh, well. One complimentary glass doesn't make us spongers.

EDITH
Let's debate that when we're on our third! *(they both chuckle as they raise their glasses and look over at CECIL)* Cheers! *(CECIL nods, then raises his glass in their direction. As he does, Sir John taps him on the shoulder)*

SIR JOHN
Peter, old man, is it too much if I order another little snifter?

CECIL
Of course not, Sir John. Have a double if you wish.

SIR JOHN
That's most kind. *(SIR JOHN signals to the barman to bring him a whisky soda, then turns back to CECIL)* That's very good of you, old bean.

CECIL
Anytime, after all, unlike you. I can afford it.

SIR JOHN
Ouch! That's rubbing salt in the wound. I admit it. I certainly can't afford doubles, not these days, anyway. Too many expensive divorces, not to mention those damn parties.

CECIL
(CECIL smirks) It seems most people here have squandered their money needlessly.

SIR JOHN
Well, when you're young, you never think about what happens when you get older, do you? You'd never dream you'd end up in a place like this, thanks to charity.

CECIL
No, I didn't.

SIR JOHN
There we are, then. None of us does.

CECIL
I said I didn't.

SIR JOHN
Yes, I heard.

CECIL
I meant I didn't end up here like the rest of you. Skint.

SIR JOHN
(SIR JOHN pauses and looks at CECIL) Yes, I was going to ask you about that. Look, without meaning to be rude. It's very kind and all that, but where d'you get the money to be so generous to everyone?

CECIL
Without not meaning to be rude. That's my business.

SIR JOHN
(SIR JOHN appears upset by his remark) Yes, of course, it is. But while we're on the subject. How did you manage to get in here?

CECIL
Through the entrance, like everyone else.

SIR JOHN
(SIR JOHN pauses) To be perfectly candid, I can't remember working with you. And I've worked with countless actors in my time. Most of us here know each other from working together or by our professional reputations.

CECIL
You surprise me. You nearly offered me a lift once in your Rolls Royce.

SIR JOHN
If I had the Rolls, that must have been during the good old days. *(laughs)* When I had money.

CECIL
It was. I also attended quite a few of your parties.

SIR JOHN
Did you, now?

CECIL
Yes, and I can honestly say, they were hard work. *(CECIL takes a gold cigarette case from his jacket)*

SIR JOHN
What a beautiful case. I used to have one, just like it.

CECIL
(CECIL quickly puts it back in his pocket) Go and get me some cigarettes, will you? I've run out. Here's a tenner, you can keep the change.

SIR JOHN
Of course, old boy! *(SIR JOHN goes to sip his drink)*

CECIL
(CECIL pulls SIR JOHN closer and takes the drink out of his hand, grabs him by his lapels) I said, bugger off and get my cigarettes. Otherwise, no more free drinkies! *(SIR JOHN looks shocked)*

EDITH
(EDITH and DAME SYBIL are watching) D'you see that? He seems to be getting very aggressive with Sir John.

DAME SYBIL
I did, indeed.

EDITH
I get the feeling there's something fishy about him. Don't you think?

DAME SYBIL
I do, and I'd love to know what.

EDITH
Me too.

DAME SYBIL
There is definitely more to our Mr Brock than meets the eye.

BLACKOUT

ACT I SCENE II

LANDLADY'S HOUSE. DAYTIME. 1945.

THE HALLWAY OF A SHABBY-LOOKING HOUSE. THE BELL RINGS. THE LANDLADY APPEARS AND OPENS THE FRONT-DOOR. A YOUNG CECIL IS STANDING ON THE DOORSTEP SPORTING A TRILBY HAT, A MACINTOSH AND CARRYING A SUITCASE.

CECIL
Hello, I'm looking for a room.

PEGGY
How long would you be wanting it for?

CECIL
I'm not sure, a week or two. Maybe more.

PEGGY
Then you'd better come in. *(CECIL enters)* I only have a double.

CECIL
That's okay.

PEGGY
It's a lovely room on this floor. It used to be our room before my husband died.

CECIL
I'm sorry to hear that.

PEGGY
He was killed in the blitz fighting the fires.

CECIL
I take it he was a fireman.

PEGGY
He was at that. But you have to move on, don't you?

CECIL
I guess you do

PEGGY
It'll be six shillings a week, and it's a week in advance. By the way, I'm Mrs O'Brian, but they call me Peggy. And what is your name?

CECIL
Cecil.

PEGGY
Cecil, is it?

CECIL
Cecil O'Docherty

PEGGY
Irish? So am I. Where in Ireland are you from?

CECIL
County Galway originally, but I moved to Dublin before I came here.

PEGGY
I take it. It'll be your first time in England.

CECIL
Yes, how did you know?

PEGGY
What with the war on. It wouldn't have been a good time to come before.

CECIL
I heard the bombing was terrible.

PEGGY
Aye, it was at that. And to think, it's only been three months since the Gerries surrendered. That's when you should have been here, VE Day. Now that's what you'd call a party.

CECIL
It must have been amazing.

PEGGY
Just one big street party from John O'Groats to Lands End.

CECIL
Was it indeed?

PEGGY
People were singing and dancing. Complete strangers, kissing each other in the street. *(PEGGY winks)* and a lot more besides. You'll never see a party like that again.

CECIL
I'm sorry I missed it. *(PEGGY opens the door to his room. CECIL briefly looks inside)* I'll take it. *(CECIL hands her the rent, and Peggy gives him a key and then points out the bathroom)*

PEGGY
The toilet and bathing facilities are down the hall. So what is it you do for work?

CECIL
Actor. I'm an actor. Well, I want to be.

PEGGY
An actor, is it? You are one? Or you want to be one?

CECIL
I'm going to be one.

PEGGY
Then you've come to the right place. I get a lot of you theatricals here. I was in show business myself.

CECIL
You were in show business?

PEGGY
Yes, before coming over here and meeting my husband.

CECIL
Did you work as an actress?

PEGGY
No! Take a guess. *(PEGGY hitches her skirt up to the Knee)*

CECIL
(CECIL looks surprised) A dancer?

PEGGY
You got it in one! *(she lowers her skirt)*

CECIL
Why did you stop?

PEGGY
Love dear. I got pregnant at eighteen. So I had no choice and got married that same year and moved in here with my husband.

CECIL
So a happy ending, eh?

PEGGY
Not really. I lost the child. She was stillborn. He never got over it. Especially when the doctors said I couldn't have any more children.

CECIL
I'm sorry.

PEGGY
It's all in the past now. Twelve years ago this spring. Oh, well. What's done is done. Now, you'll be opposite Peter. He's also an actor, so I am sure you two will find a lot to chat about. *(At that moment, a handsome young man, similar in build to CECIL appears)*

PEGGY
Talk of the devil. Peter, say hello to Cecil, he's just arrived from Ireland. And like yourself, *(she winks)* he's also a lesbian.

PETER
(Peter grins) I think you mean thespian.

PEGGY
I know that, I'm just kidding with you. You can call yourselves whatever fancy names you'd like. *(PETER AND CECIL smile as they shake hands)* Peter, Cecil's fresh off the boat, so help him find his feet. You know, give him a few pointers about how to get into acting. Now I'd best be leaving you two boys to it. I've work to do. *(as PEGGY exits. CECIL just stares at PETER and grins)*

PETER
So you're an actor too?

CECIL
I'm going to try my luck in that direction.

PETER
An Irish hobbledehoy, eh?

CECIL
And what's that supposed to mean?

PETER
If I'm not mistaken, it stands for an awkward adolescent youth. And, in your case, an Irish one.

CECIL
So, if I'm an awkward adolescent youth at twenty-eight, how old

does that make you?

PETER
Twenty-one… Just.

CECIL
So, neither of us is exactly an adolescent. And what have you got
against the Irish?

PETER
Me? Nothing. It's just your accent.

CECIL
My accent?

PETER
It's charming but not the easiest to understand.

CECIL
Oh, is that right? And what business is it of yours?

PETER
None at all.

CECIL
Then mind your business. *(CECIL turns to go into his room)*

PETER
I didn't mean any offence by it. It was Peggy who suggested I give
you some pointers.

CECIL
Pointers?

PETER
Forget it. I was only trying to be helpful.

CECIL
Come off it. You were patronising me.

PETER
No, I wasn't.

CECIL
You Brits are all the same. I would have thought, now this bloody war is over. You would have learned your lesson. You don't rule the waves anymore!

PETER
Look if I've annoyed you. Maybe we should do what they do in the movies?

CECIL
Which is what?

PETER
You know. Rewind things back to the bit where we were shaking hands, and you were smiling? *(PETER puts his hand out for CECIL to shake. CECIL pauses before taking PETER'S hand. He then looks at PETER and smiles)* Now we've got that out of the way. You'd best come in and have a cup of tea. Oh, and I have some really nice cake left over from my birthday.

PETER
Happy birthday.

CECIL
That was nearly six months ago.

PETER
It must be a bit stale by now, then.

CECIL
Not at all. *(CECIL follows PETER into his room. The room is basic, with a double bed, a washstand and an armchair that has seen better days. There is a gas fire for heating and a small hob to boil things)* Look, I was only trying to be helpful.

CECIL
Helpful? In what way?

PETER
You know, make some suggestions on how to go about getting acting work. Unless, of course, you already have contacts in that field.

CECIL
No, I can't say I have. I'd be grateful for a few tips. What do you suggest?

PETER
For a start. Your name is Cecil, right?

CECIL
So?

PETER
What's your full name?

CECIL
Cecil Patrick Murphy O'Docherty. D'you know what Dochartaigh

means in Gaelic?

PETER
No.

CECIL
Hurtful.

PETER
(PETER surprised) Really? Then I'd best be more careful.

CECIL
Don't worry. That's only to my enemies. So, what's your surname?

PETER
Piotr Wisniewski.

CECIL
That's a mouthful.

PETER
That's why I had to change it.

CECIL
Where does that name come from?

PETER
My dad's parents were Polish. But he was born here.

CECIL
And your mam?

PETER
She was English.

CECIL
Was?

PETER
She died in an air raid four years ago.

CECIL
I'm sorry. It must be tough.

PETER
It is.

CECIL
And your dad?

PETER
He's in the R.A.F. based abroad. So I lived with my aunt Daisy in the country.

CECIL
How long have you been in London, then?

PETER
On and off since I was sixteen.

CECIL
So, what made you go into showbusiness?

PETER
My dad is an actor. *(chuckles)* So it seemed a good idea at the time.

CECIL
At the time. Why Did you go off the idea, then?

PETER
No, I haven't at all! It's just it's not easy in the theatre.

CECIL
Why?

PETER
All kinds of reasons. For a start, it helps if you did what I did.

CECIL
Which is?

PETER
Anglicise your name. You have to a name that slips off the tongue.

CECIL
Like what?

PETER
(PETER makes the tea and hands CECIL a cup and a slice of cake)
Well, take mine, for instance. Piotr is Peter in Polish. But anglicised and coupled with Brock, an abbreviation of Brockenhurst, the village I grew up in. It rolls off the tongue and sounds as English as a game of cricket.

CECIL
Aye, it does at that. *(CECIL tries the cake)* You're right. It's not stale.

PETER
Keeping it in this tin helps preserve it. It's very moreish. My aunt makes it with a lot of honey. It's a bit too sweet for me.

CECIL
Not at all, it's very nice. *(winks at PETER)* I always say the sweeter, the better.

PETER
(PETER seems embarrassed) Anyway, nearly everybody does it.

CECIL
Do they, indeed?

PETER
I meant anglicise their names, especially if they want to become a film star. Don't forget Francis Gumm became Judy Garland and Doris Kappelhof...

CECIL
Doris?

PETER
She became Doris Day. And what about Archibald Leach, Bernard Schwartz and Issur Danielovitch? You must have heard of them.

CECIL
No, I can't say I have.

PETER
Better known to you and me as Cary Grant, Tony Curtis and Kirk Douglas. And there are so many others who have done it.

CECIL
Is this true? Or are you taking the piss?

PETER
Of course, it's true! Do you think they would have made it otherwise? Mind you, in the theatre. It's more about articulation and diction. So you might have to change your accent, too.

CECIL
And while I'm at it, perhaps you'd like me to shave my head as well?

PETER
No, that would be going too far unless the part calls for it.

CECIL
Oh, would it now? You want to change my name and how I speak, but shaving my head is going too far?

PETER
Yes, I think so, don't you?

CECIL
(CECIL laughs) Unlike your other suggestions, at least it would grow back!

PETER
(PETER smiles) I suppose.

CECIL
You've got the cheek of the devil. I give you that.

PETER
What do you think Sir Laurence Olivier or Sir John Gielgud would have sounded like? If they had attempted Shakespeare without having had elocution lessons at drama school.

CECIL
Those two must be famous, right? *(CECIL helps himself to more cake)*

PETER
Very. Look, if you like, I can try to help you there.

CECIL
Help me where?

PETER
Improve your diction.

CECIL
And how would you do that?

PETER
Even though I was born here, I also had to take elocution lessons.

CECIL
Elocution?

PETER
I didn't always speak like this. *(PETER does a South London accent)* I had to learn how to talk proper. I was brought up in sarf London. *(switches back to his normal voice)* So you see, I was given elocution lessons to learn how to speak correctly.

CECIL
That's amazing. The way you just spoke. It's like I'm talking to a different person.

PETER
Exactly. That's the point. My dad did the same.

CECIL
But why would he do that?

PETER
He wouldn't have made it in this business otherwise. *(PETER slips back into a south London accent)* Especially wiv a Peckham accent? *(in his normal voice)* Who knows, one day, someone might. But these days, it's King's English if you want to become a leading man.

CECIL
I take it he's a successful actor, then?

PETER
My dad? Very. As far as he's been the lead in several films. But let's not talk about him.

CECIL
Why? You don't get on?

PETER
We get on very well. Look, Dad sent me this watch for my birthday.

CECIL
(PETER shows CECIL the watch) Nice, it looks expensive. So why don't you want to talk about him?

PETER
I intend to make it on my own in this business. Not because my dad is famous.

CECIL
I see.

PETER
Anyway, as I was saying, elocution lessons might help soften your accent a bit. *(PETER chuckles)* I'll be fun, I could be your Professor Higgins.

CECIL
Professor who?

PETER
You know, as in Pygmalion, written by your fellow countryman, Bernard Shaw?

CECIL
(confused) Ah, Yes, of course. *(CECIL helps himself to more cake)*

PETER
We can work on some audition pieces together.

CECIL
Auditions pieces?

PETER
You know, little vignettes from Dickens and Shakespeare to something modern. To show your range when you go up for a job.

CECIL
That sounds good.

PETER
It'll be fun. And besides, I'm not working. So it'll help pass the time.

CECIL
So I take it there's not much work about then?

PETER
Plenty. But I'm still waiting for my Equity card to arrive.

CECIL
What's that?

PETER
It's the actors union card. You can't get a job without one.

CECIL
Oh, I see. *(CECIL takes the last piece of the cake)*.

PETER
(CECIL goes to munch on it) Gosh, you've finished it!

CECIL
Is that a problem?

PETER
Not really, it's just that, what with the rationing.

CECIL
I'm sorry. I forgot about that. We don't have rationing in Ireland.

PETER
Lucky you. Don't worry. I'll write to my aunt and tell her to bake some more when she can. *(chuckles)* Looks like we are going to need them. You've certainly got a sweet tooth. I'll give you that.

CECIL

(chuckles) I did warn you. Now, these lessons of yours. How much would you charge?

PETER

(PETER smiles) Well, as we're practically roommates. I'm sure between us, we'll think of something.

CECIL

(CECIL puts his arm on PETER'S shoulder) Yes. I'm sure we will.

LIGHT FADE

ACT I. SCENE III

A COUPLE OF MONTHS LATER. PETER'S ROOM EARLY EVENING

PETER

(CECIL and PETER sit cross-legged on the bed, dressed only in their underwear) You're a quick learner. I'll give you that. In just over, what is it, eight or nine weeks? And you already sound more English than I do. Granted, a bit over the top at times, but believable.

CECIL

As long as it's believable, that's all that matters.

PETER

It certainly is. It's a bit creepy. You sound exactly like me.

CECIL
I must say, all that tongue-twister stuff. 'Shut up the Shutters and sit in the shop nonsense.' It sounded all very innocent until you made me say it faster and faster.

PETER
(PETER laughs) That was the general idea. They do say when things are fun, it's easier to learn.

CECIL
It's certainly been fun. *(CECIL slaps PETER'S thigh)* But be honest, do I sound as posh as you?

PETER
If I'm honest, even more so. Well done.

CECIL
Credit where it's due. It's down to you. You've been very patient.

PETER
I'm afraid patience is something I'm fast running out of.

CECIL
You should have told me. I'm sorry.

PETER
I didn't mean you. No. It's this waiting around for my union ticket. What's so annoying is I could be going to tons of auditions. But there's no point; they won't employ me without it.

CECIL
At least it's coming.

PETER
But it's taken so long. It's reason enough for you to give up acting before you start.

CECIL
I could never do that! I've got a real taste for it now.

PETER
Do you realise how long it's taken me to get this card? Three years!

CECIL
I don't think I can wait that long.

PETER
I'm afraid you'll have to, and it may take even longer. An Equity card is like gold dust.

CECIL
How did you get yours?

PETER
I was A.S.M. in a repertory company at the Palace Theatre North-ampton.

CECIL
A.S.M?

PETER
Assistant Stage Manager. It's just a grand title to disguise the fact you're the general dog's body. I was only on stage to sweep it when the curtain was down. And when the curtain was up, I was usually off stage, prompting ageing actors to try and remember their lines.

CECIL
At least it was a means to an end.

PETER
True. And you can glean a lot from watching the actors perform night after night. It's a great way to learn your craft.

CECIL
So you didn't do any acting yourself, then?

PETER
Eventually, just small parts, but not until my second year. As I said, it took a lot of time.

CECIL
And? *(CECIL strokes PETER'S bare shoulder)* Go on.

PETER
There's nothing more to tell. As you see, I'm still stuck here waiting for my card to arrive.

CECIL
There must be an easier way.

PETER
(PETER laughs) Short of murder. I'm afraid there isn't. Now, enough about me. I want to hear about you for a change.

CECIL
But Why?

PETER
Come off it. You spend more time in this bed than in your own. By

now, I know every inch of your body, yet little to nothing about you.

CECIL
What more is there to say?

PETER
Tell me about your childhood. What made you want to go into acting?

CECIL
That's easy. Poverty. My parents have a smallholding near Galway, where I was born. My father and mother worked hard, so we always had enough to eat, but there were no luxuries, far from it.

PETER
It doesn't sound that bad. At least you had your family around.

CECIL
I did at that. And they were good to me. But I want more out of life.

PETER
Is that what made you decide to become an actor?

CECIL
No, that was when I moved to Dublin. I met this old actor in a pub who said I had a good face for acting. After a few pints, he invited me back to his place and said that I could stay as long as I wanted

PETER
(cynically) Oh, yes? Come on, the truth!

CECIL
Well, let's put it this way. He didn't charge me any rent, and in re-

turn, I helped him out when he wasn't busy, if you get my meaning?

PETER
(Peter grins) I think I do.

CECIL
Mind you, one day. He went too far. He crossed the line and tried to stick his tongue down my throat.

PETER
Really? So what did you do?

CECIL
So I stuck my fist down his.

PETER
You didn't? The poor man. *(PETER seems shocked)* You didn't really, did you?

CECIL
It did the trick. He never tried that again. Even so, I had to move out.

PETER
You can't blame him for throwing you out. You're lucky he didn't call the police.

CECIL
No, he never said a word. He couldn't. The problem was, after a while, his corpse made the flat stink. So I had no choice but to leave.

PETER
That is disgusting! *(PETER nervously chuckles)* You are joking, right?

CECIL
Don't be so daft. Of course, I'm joking.

PETER
At times, I never know whether to take you seriously or not.

CECIL
(CECIL laughs) D'you really think I'd be telling you if I had done it? Just look at the expression on your face. It's priceless. *(CECIL points to PETER'S reflection in a mirror on the chest of drawer)*

PETER
I know, stupid me, I'm so bloody gullible.

CECIL
But seriously, you should have seen his place. Full of signed photographs of the famous people he had worked with.

PETER
What was his name?

CECIL
His name doesn't matter. But his stories of hanging out with film stars and going to all these fancy parties are what's important. Also, I couldn't believe actors get paid money just for spouting other people's words. That's when I thought to myself. I want some of that, and I don't care what it takes to get it.

PETER
That might not be as easy or as glamorous as you think.

CECIL
Now, why would you go and say a thing like that?

PETER
Because acting takes skill and dedication, but most importantly, talent to bring written words to life and make the characters believable. True, you might work with famous actors, but it doesn't mean you'll get to hang out with them. They usually only hobnob in their circles. *(PETER caresses CECIL'S bare leg, then goes to kiss him on the lips. As he does, CECIL angrily pushes him off the bed and rubs his mouth with the back of his hand)*

CECIL
That's one thing I can't be dealing with, men kissing men.

PETER
(looks frightened) So you weren't joking?

CECIL
What? Of course I was. It's just I draw the line at that.

PETER
I just don't understand you. You spend half the night sticking your tongue everywhere else, but kissing is forbidden.

CECIL
What we do is just sex. l told you I'm straight.

PETER
(nervously) Okay. I'm sorry, I wasn't thinking. *(PETER stands up)*

CECIL
Don't ever try that again. Otherwise, I'll get nasty. And I don't want to do that because I like you.

PETER
I like you too.

CECIL
Maybe, too much for your own good. If that Peggy woman had walked in just then, she'd have called the coppers.

PETER
I'm sorry.

CECIL
Remember, if we were caught. It could mean prison.

PETER
I said I was sorry.

CECIL
It's getting chilly in here. Go and light the fire, and don't blow us all up. *(PETER takes some matches and ignites the gas fire. Then gets back on the bed. CECIL grins)* Now, where were we? *(At that moment, there is a knock on the door, and they both freeze. PETER whispers)*

PETER
What do we do?

CECIL
Is that door locked?

PETER
Yes.

CECIL
It's probably just Peggy wanting the rent money. Keep quiet, and She'll go away. *(they wait for a while and then we hear footsteps fading into the distance)* There we are. She's gone.

PETER
Look, she's slipped something under the door.

CECIL
(CECIL laughs) Probably your rent bill!

PETER
(PETER jumps off the bed and opens the envelope, and then yelps) I don't believe it! It's come at last.

CECIL
Is it what I think it is?

PETER
Yes, my Equity card! *(PETER waves it in the air, and then he kisses it)* Just look at it. See, I told you, gold dust!

CECIL
Let me see it. *(PETER hands it to CECIL)* Now, this is a cause for a celebration.

PETER
It certainly is. And the timing couldn't be more perfect. Now I can go to that audition next week.

CECIL
What audition?

PETER
This one in The Stage newspaper. *(PETER shows CECIL)* It's for a national tour. They are looking for somebody with dark hair in their early twenties. It's a pity you don't have one of these. *(PETER waves his card and teases CECIL)* You'd be perfect for the part. But then, to me, you will always be perfect.

CECIL
In that case, tonight, to celebrate us both being perfect and both perfect for the part. I'm taking you out for a drink. No, correction. I'm taking you for lots of drinks!

PETER
But you know I don't drink.

CECIL
Ah, come on. Are you a man or a mouse?

PETER
Mouse.

CECIL
Then tonight, I'm going to make you a man.

PETER
Alright then, but just half a shandy. And I'm buying the drinks. You're not working, remember.

CECIL
Neither are you.

PETER
No worries. See. My dad sends me money to tie me over.
(PETER goes to the draw and brings out an envelope full of cash.

Takes out some notes and puts it back)

CECIL
Now that's what I call a great dad to have. What's his name again?

PETER
I told you I'd rather not say. If I did, you'd recognise it.

CECIL
What's wrong with that?

PETER
How many times do we have to go through this? I want to be an actor in my own right. Anyway, tonight, the drinks are on me.

CECIL
I insist we split the bill. It'll be my investment.

PETER
Investment?

CECIL
In you. And for your lessons in teaching me to be as close to Peter Brock as is mentally and physically possible. *(PETER hugs CECIL)*

PETER
Aah, Cecil, you really can be so sweet when you want to be.

LIGHTS FADE

LATER THE SAME EVENING. PETER'S ROOM

The door opens, and CECIL and PETER stagger in. PETER is barely able to walk. CECIL helps him onto the bed, where he passes out. CECIL removes PETER'S wristwatch before systematically going through the chest of draws and taking the envelope stuffed with cash. He then takes an almost empty bottle of scotch out of his pocket, wipes it with a cloth and puts it in PETER'S hand before placing it on the bedside table. CECIL goes to the door and removes the key. Carefully holding it by the tip, he wipes clean the bow before putting it in PETER'S hand and gently squeezing it. After wiping the tip of the key, he wraps it in his handkerchief. CECIL then picks up the Equity card and slips it into his pocket. Finally, CECIL goes to the fireplace and turns on the gas fire but doesn't light it. He switches off the light and leaves, locking the door from the outside.

BLACKOUT

ACT I SCENE IV

MORNING SEVERAL HOURS LATER. HALLWAY.

CECIL
(CECIL is in the hall shouting down the stairs) Mrs O'Brian! Wake up! Mrs O'Brian. It's an emergency! Mrs O'Brian.

PEGGY
(PEGGY enters) What is it? Do you realise what time it is? *(she looks at the watch on his wrist)* It's six a.m.!

CECIL
Tell me if you can smell gas.

PEGGY
(PEGGY sniffs the air) I can. Where on earth's it coming from?

CECIL
From Peter's room. I've banged on his door, but he's not answering.

PEGGY
Try again.

CECIL
(CECIL bangs on PETER'S door) Peter? Are you in there? *(CECIL knocks again)* Maybe he went out early.

PEGGY
Don't just stand there. Open the door.

CECIL
It's locked. What d'you want me to do?

PEGGY
(PEGGY tries to open it) Break it down, of course!

CECIL
Okay, then stand back. *(CECIL breaks down the door. As he enters the bedroom, he calls to PEGGY)* Don't come in here. Not until I open a window. *(CECIL quickly unwraps the key whilst keeping the bow end covered. CECIL places it back in the lock from the inside. Then turns off the gas fire and finally checks if PETER is still breathing before opening the window)* Peggy, you can come in now. It's safe.

PEGGY
(PEGGY enters the bedroom) Bejesus, what on earth has gone on here? *(She checks on PETER)* Peter. Come on now, wake up. *(PEG-GY waves her hand in his face like a fan)* Get some of this lovely fresh air down yer. You'll soon feel better.

CECIL
Peggy, I've already felt his pulse. I'm afraid he's no longer with us.

PEGGY
Oh, don't say that. Poor mite. How could he be so stupid as to forget to light the fire? Oh, no. You don't think?

CECIL
Think what?

PEGGY
You know... It was suicide?

CECIL
But why would he?

PEGGY
What on earth was I thinking? Of course, it wasn't suicide.

CECIL
So what do you think happened?

PEGGY
He must have switched on the fire but forgot to light it.

CECIL
(CECIL seems relieved) Yes, an accident. That sounds about right.

PEGGY
That's one good thing. At least there's been no foul play.

CECIL
Foul play? There couldn't have been. There's no other way in. *(CECIL looks out the window)* Take a look. It's a sheer drop from here down into the basement.

PEGGY
(PEGGY pats PETER'S hand) You poor little darling. *(PEGGY then takes another look around the room before opening the wardrobe)* But why would he do that?

CECIL
Do what?

PEGGY
Commit suicide. Peter was such a sensible lad. *(PEGGY opens the wardrobe)* See, everything is always so neat and in its place.

CECIL
True, he was very fussy about his things.

PEGGY
(PEGGY opens the chest of drawers) See how tidy everything is? His scripts are on one side, and all his correspondence is neatly-placed on the other. Everything is so nice and neat. It doesn't make sense it being an accident.

CECIL
Why?

PEGGY
For him to forget to light the fire? He is meticulous.

CECIL
Was.

PEGGY
Don't be so heartless.

CECIL
By the looks of it, it was too much of this. *(CECIL points to the empty whiskey bottle)*

PEGGY
What a Silly boy. That's why I don't allow drinking in the rooms. That's another odd thing. I never knew Peter drank.

CECIL
I never actually saw him drink. But you can always tell a drinker. You can smell it on their breath.

PEGGY
Don't remind me. My husband would roll in most nights stinking of alcohol. If I'd had lit a cigarette near him, we'd have both gone up in flames.

CECIL
It's sad to think that Peter was a secret drinker. But you can never tell with people, can you?

PEGGY
Indeed, you can't. Oh, well. I'd best ring for an ambulance and the police.

CECIL
Yes, you should.

PEGGY
(PEGGY looks down at the floor by the bed, picks up a piece of underwear, and hands it to CECIL with a knowing look) Yours, I believe?

CECIL
I don't think so.

PEGGY
Come on, McGrath's of Dublin is on the tag. Don't you think, running this place, I haven't seen it all before? There's no use trying to pull the wool over my eyes.

CECIL
What d'you mean?

PEGGY
If the police had found these by his bed. I could have been done for running an immoral house. And I don't need that sort of scandal on top of everything else. The neighbours will have enough to gossip about as it is.

CECIL
I hope you're not insinuating...

PEGGY
Then how else did your underwear get there? Walk?

CECIL
But I'm into women. *(CECIL Looks worried)* You've got it all wrong.

PEGGY
(cynically) Have I now?

CECIL
People always jump to the wrong conclusions when they don't know the full facts.

PEGGY
You're so right. Because there's me thinking that you may have had a hand in this business.

CECIL
Meaning?

PEGGY
Peter's death.

CECIL
Why on earth would you?

PEGGY
Perhaps Peter was going to reveal your little secret.

CECIL
What secret?

PEGGY
Now, what is the medical term for it? You know, when you bat for both sides.

CECIL
Me? *(CECIL smirks)* Bisexual?

PEGGY
That's the word that comes to mind.

CECIL
You got to be kidding.

PEGGY
I always suspected my husband was like that. But then, you can't always tell with men, can you?

CECIL
I wouldn't know.

PEGGY
But I could tell you were one. The first day you arrived here. It was the way you looked at Peter.

CECIL
The way I looked at him?

PEGGY
As you shook his hand, you never took your eyes off him.

CECIL
It was just a firm, friendly handshake, that's all.

PEGGY
Come off it, after that first day. Except for using the bathroom, You barely left his room.

CECIL
There's a perfectly innocent answer to that. I was too exhausted.

PEGGY
Now, why does that not surprise me?

CECIL
I meant from all that studying, acting out plays and audition pieces.

PEGGY
From the noises I heard coming out of here, they must have been physically very demanding.

CECIL
They were, and that's what you must have heard.

CECIL
Peter really helped me improve myself.

PEGGY
Bless him. He certainly achieved that. You've become quite the English gentleman now, haven't you?

CECIL
Yes, and I'm very grateful to him for that.

PEGGY
And me? Are you going to show me some gratitude?

CECIL
Yes, of course. I'm very grateful.

PEGGY
For your own sake, I hope you are. Because, like everything, it all goes back to the evils of money.

CECIL
And sadly, I don't have any.

PEGGY
Now, there is the craic. I think you do. In fact, I know you do. And if I'm right. It should be around three pounds.

CECIL
Three pounds?

PEGGY
The money you stole from Peter. I'll be about three pounds, give or take the odd few shillings.

CECIL
I didn't take any money from him.

PEGGY
No. You took the envelope from that drawer.

CECIL
(CECIL takes her hand) Now, why would you even think that?

PEGGY
(PEGGY looks at his watch) The fact you're wearing his watch helps. I must say the police are taking their time. You would have thought death would have counted as an emergency.

CECIL
But then, there's nothing more they can do when they get here, is there?

PEGGY
Investigate?

CECIL
I suppose.

PEGGY
At least it's given us time to have this little chat to clear the air. But whether I should go for accidental death, suicide or foul play, of course, in the end, the choice would be yours.

CECIL
Mine?

PEGGY
When the police ask me questions, I'd hate to say the wrong thing. In case it might influence their investigation in any way.

CECIL
I'm sure they'll just come to the same conclusion as I did. Accidentally death.

PEGGY
Ah, but policeman's careers are built on suspicion. Who knows, they might even suspect murder. You know what they are like.

CECIL
Murder? Come now. How could anyone have gotten in here? As I said, there's no way through that window without the risk of breaking your neck or impaling yourself on the railings. And don't forget the door was locked from the inside.

PEGGY
It was. But then I'm sure you could make anything believable, convince people the colour black is white.

CECIL
But black is not a colour. It's a shade.

PEGGY
There we are. See, you've convinced me. Of course, it's that charm of yours that does it. And, if I say so myself, it also helps that you're a handsome lad.

CECIL
Does it indeed? Well, if we're paying each other compliments, did I ever tell you you're an attractive woman?

PEGGY
Oh, get away with you. No more of your malarky now.

CECIL
From that first day when I stood on that step, and you opened that door, all I could see were those big blue eyes, bluer than the morning sky they reflected. I thought to myself. She's beautiful. Pity, she's my landlady. I'd like to know her better.

PEGGY
(PEGGY gets flustered) Get away with yer. You certainly have a way with words. I'll give you that.

CECIL
So do you.

PEGGY
Now, be serious. Before anyone arrives, be honest with me now. Did you, in any way, have a hand in this poor boy's demise?

CECIL
(CECIL grabs PEGGY with both hands and looks into her eyes) Of course, I didn't! How could you even think such a thing?

PEGGY
Then, swear to me on your life.

CECIL
Why would I harm him? It doesn't make any sense.

PEGGY
I suppose it doesn't. But a scandal like that could ruin me. So I hope for my sake you're telling me the truth.

CECIL
(CECIL gently strokes her cheek and smiles) Peggy, look at me. Take a good, close look. D'you think I'm not telling you the truth?

PEGGY
I'm inclined to believe you, but I'm sure thousands wouldn't.

CECIL
But what if the police think something more sinister happened?

PEGGY
(PEGGY pats CECIL'S cheek) Let's cross that bridge when we come to it.

CECIL
I'm sure if you steer them in the right direction, that should clear up any doubts.

PEGGY
Then I might just do that. For a price, that is.

CECIL
And what would that be?

PEGGY
I'll let you keep the watch, but you can hand over that money you took from that drawer. *(police siren in the background)* You best make up your mind now. Petty pilfering is one thing. I admit to hav ing been found guilty of it myself. But if you're not telling me the truth, murder is another.

CECIL
But you just said you believed me?

PEGGY
And I do. Ninety-nine per cent. Let's just say I'm hedging my bets. Now, you'd better decide quickly. Because, if I'm correct, that is a police siren I can hear.

CECIL
I take it you're aware this is blackmail? *(CECIL hands her the money)*

PEGGY
Yes, I suppose it is. But then, if you're lying to me, unlike murder, it's not a hanging offence.

CECIL
They'd have difficulty proving it.

PEGGY
Maybe. But what doesn't add up. Peter had just received his Equity card. So, he had everything to live for. So it couldn't be suicide.

CECIL
Then, obviously, it was an accident. Peter had too many drinks celebrating, then turned on the gas but forgot to light the fire.

PEGGY
Yes, but you taking his card. Now the police might find that highly suspicious. So for your sake. I hope you're innocent.

CECIL
What card are you on about?

PEGGY
The card I slipped under that door last night. I can't see it anywhere.

CECIL
How did you know what it was?

PEGGY
By opening the envelope, of course.

CECIL
You know that's a criminal offence?

PEGGY
So is stealing Peter's identity.

CECIL,
His identity?

PEGGY
How else did you propose to use the card?

CECIL
Come on, Peggy, you have to look at it sensibly. It's sad, but
Peter didn't need it anymore. He was already dead.

PEGGY
That's a cruel way of putting it.

CECIL
And for me to get into Equity, it could take two or three years.

PEGGY
Will it now?

CECIL
And that card will only end up in the rubbish bin.

PEGGY
But for you to be able to use it, you'd have to become him.

CECIL
Of course not, it's just his stage name.

PEGGY
Oh, I see. So, you wouldn't be stealing Peter's real name, just a
made-up one?

CECIL
That's right! One he's never even used. So apart from you and I, no one will ever know.

PEGGY
Well, I suppose, if it wasn't his real name. I can't see what harm it can do. And, as you say, it's no use to Peter anymore, poor little bugger. *(Doorbell rings)* At last. We'll continue this later. But for now, you'd best keep out of the way. Go to your room. Lock the door and stay very quiet until the police have left. Come down to me later. I'll make us something to eat.

LIGHTS FADE

ACT I SCENE V

LANDLADY'S FLAT. LATER THAT EVENING
(PEGGY opens the door, and CECIL walks straight into the centre of the living room)

CECIL
What happened? There was a lot of commotion. They weren't looking for me, were they?

PEGGY
Don't be so daft.

CECIL
What did they say? Were they suspicious?

PEGGY
All in good time. Now, calm down. And I'll get you a nice cold beer from the pantry.

CECIL
Calm down? I've been locked in my room since early this morning. I couldn't even sneak out to the toilet.

PEGGY
I hope you didn't use the sink. I know how lazy you boys can be.

CECIL
I had no choice.

PEGGY
Oh, well. Needs must, I suppose. *(PEGGY gets CECIL a beer, pours it into a glass and hands it to CECIL)* Get this down yer. It'll calm your nerves. A nice drop of stout never did anyone any harm.

CECIL
(CECIL takes a gulp) So there's nothing I should be worried about?

PEGGY
(a clock on the mantlepiece chimes) Would you look at that? It's already eight o'clock. You arrived in good time for some dinner.

CECIL
Peggy, please. Do I have to beg you to tell me what happened?

PEGGY
Don't be so daft. But before we get to all that. Sit down and get a warm meal inside you. You look like you've seen a ghost.

CECIL
It was just all that noise, and not knowing what was happening....

PEGGY
Just calm down and sit at the table. *(PEGGY ladles some stew into a bowl and serves it to CECIL)* It's been an exhausting day for me, too, remember?

CECIL
Of course, it has. It's just I've been on tenterhooks waiting for them to leave.

PEGGY
I know you have. It's only natural, Cecil. Or am I calling you Peter now?

CECIL
I suggest starting, as I mean to go on. Peter will suit me fine.

PEGGY
And I have every confidence that it will. *(PEGGY lifts her glass)* Now, how's your meal?

CECIL
It looks delicious. It's just I'm too wound up to eat.

PEGGY
Now that's a shame, as it's a good Irish stew in your honour. I'll do you a deal. I'll tell you what happened if you eat something.

CECIL
Okay.

PEGGY
Well, the ambulance men arrived first and confirmed Peter was dead.

CECIL
We already knew that.

PEGGY
Then, the police arrived and ushered me out of the room. They were in there for ages investigating what happened.

CECIL
What did they say?

PEGGY
They wouldn't tell me anything. Then someone from the coroner's office arrived and took the body away.

CECIL
Did they ask you any questions?

PEGGY
I'm coming to that. Now, sup up. It was pandemonium, what with people coming and going. It was hard to keep track of who was who.

CECIL
Okay, I get it. But what questions did they ask you?

PEGGY
Funny enough, not many.

CECIL
Not many? So what did they ask?

PEGGY
Oh, just what Peter's full name was. Of course, I gave them that Polish name of his.

CECIL
Nothing else? Didn't they ask anything else?

PEGGY
Only what sort of a lad was he? I said he was a lovely lad, quiet and no trouble. They also asked if he had any friends. So I told them he was a bit of a loner. They then went through his documents, and that was about it.

CECIL
Did they give a hint as to what they thought happened?

PEGGY
As far as I can gather, they thought it could have been an accident. But they would only know that once they have the coroner's report.

CECIL
That doesn't sound promising.

PEGGY
Oh, go on with you. It's nothing for you to worry your head about. It's just routine, that's all. It'll all be over sooner than you think. Now, let's down to more practical matters.

CECIL
What practical matters?

PEGGY
Your room.

CECIL
My room? What's that got to do with anything?

PEGGY
Peter's room might be out of bounds for a while. Which means I'll need to rent yours instead.

CECIL
But you can't do that. Where would I go? Why not one of the other tenants? The old boy on the top floor, for instance?

PEGGY
Mr Gregson? Oh, no, I could never do that. He's been here for years.

CECIL
Then what about the one opposite him?

PEGGY
Do you mean Mrs Riley? She's no trouble. She's hardly ever here. Always off to Europe or somewhere.

CECIL
Then what happens to me?

PEGGY
I've been thinking about what you said this morning. You know, about my blue eyes.

CECIL
Your eyes. What have they got to do with my room?

PEGGY
According to you, quite a lot. If you meant what you said.

CECIL
Meant what?

PEGGY
Oh, so you were just kissing the blarney stone? You said it was a pity I was your landlady. Which I took to mean...

CECIL
Oh, yes. Yes, I did. Of course, I mean it.

PEGGY
Well, it seems to me. With all this business with poor Peter, we're beyond that now. You know. Me being the landlady and you just the lodger. This terrible tragedy has brought us together.

CECIL
Of course, but...

PEGGY
There we are, then. So as you won't be needing that room anymore. You can move in here.

CECIL
Where?

PEGGY
Here. Why not? It's much more comfortable than your room. And look in there, I've got a very large double we can snuggle up in. What do you think?

CECIL
There's no reason to rush into anything, is there?

PEGGY
Oh, I think there is. The coroner's hearing could be weeks away.

CECIL
So?

PEGGY
They're bound to want me to answer more questions. And by then, I might forget what to say when I answer them. But if we were close, I'd know what to say when I answer them. It's just common sense.

CECIL
Ah, I see what you're getting at.

PEGGY
There'll be other benefits, too, of course. I could hardly be charging you rent if I'm no longer your landlady, could I?

CECIL
I suppose not. *(CECIL stands up and moves towards her)* Peggy, I think I see what you're getting at. This little arrangement could all turn out rather well for both of us.

PEGGY
I'm sure it will, at that. *(they kiss)*.

LIGHTS FADE

ACT I. SCENE VI

LANDLADY'S FLAT. EVENING SIX WEEKS LATER

CECIL
(CECIL is lying on the sofa, reading a magazine and drinking a beer. PEGGY enters) I didn't expect you until much later.

PEGGY
I can see that. Now, get your shoes off my sofa.

CECIL
(CECIL sits up) Why are you back so early?

PEGGY
They didn't need me.

CECIL
What d'you mean they didn't need you?

PEGGY
Like I said. At least give me a chance to me get my coat off. And a cup of tea would be nice.

CECIL
Of course, I'll put the kettle on.

PEGGY
I'm gasping. I was waiting for that forty-nine bus for over an hour.

CECIL
(CECIL makes the tea) Now tell me, what happened?

PEGGY
Would you believe it? I wasn't needed.

CECIL
You said that. I don't understand. You mean the coroner didn't call you as a witness?

PEGGY
Nope, or ask me any questions about Peter.

CECIL
That's odd.

PEGGY
What's odd about it?

CECIL
Telling you to go to the inquest, then not asking you any questions.

PEGGY
In the end, it was an open-and-shut case.

CECIL
I'm chomping at the bit here. Just tell me what the coroner said.

PEGGY
It wasn't so much what he said but what the police and the patholo-gist said. *(CECIL hands her a cup of tea and sits down next to her)*

CECIL
For my sake, Peggy, spit it out. I'm in mental agony here.

PEGGY
The gist of it was the police saw no signs of foul play, and neither did the pathologist.

CECIL
So? The verdict?

PEGGY
Death by misadventure. *(CECIL hugs the PEGGY and kisses her)* Careful, you're spilling me tea all down me blouse.

CECIL
I don't give a fig about your blouse. Take it off. You won't need to wear it tonight. *(CECIL gives her another kiss)*

PEGGY
Get off you, randy bugger. I'd better get some dinner on.

CECIL
Good. I'm starving. What are we having?

PEGGY
I managed to get a nice bit of scrag end. It'll boil down nicely.

CECIL
(CECIL looks at PEGGY) Oh, no. Not another old mutton neck?

PEGGY
Don't be so cheeky. It's all I can afford on my coupons.

CECIL
I forgot about the rationing. Anyhow, now the inquest is finally over. We can at last relax. I'll start going to auditions next week. There's

one playing a middle-aged psycho. I won't bother with that one, I'm too young.

PEGGY
Pity, You'd be good for that. You seem to forget. Poor Peter hasn't even been buried yet.

CECIL
I know, but I need to do something. These last few weeks have been a nightmare.

PEGGY
It hasn't been much fun for me, either.

CECIL
(CECIL hugs her) But it hasn't been all bad. We have had some fun, haven't we?

PEGGY
I suppose. *(CECIL goes to kiss her, but she pulls back)* Sometimes, I begin to wonder if you just want me for my body.

CECIL
(CECIL looks around the room) How could you even think that?

PEGGY
Ah, now get off me. I have to cook. *(PEGGY goes over to the kitchen area and starts preparing dinner. CECIL relaxes on the sofa with the Stage newspaper)* Oh, and by the way, remind me to send flowers to the lad's funeral. I was rather fond of him, you know.

LIGHTS FADE

ACT I. SCENE VII

LATE AFTERNOON. LANDLADY'S FLAT TWO MONTHS LATER.

CECIL
(CECIL enters holding a cake box) I come bearing gifts and good news.

PEGGY
A cake? Then I'd best put the kettle. So what's the good news?

CECIL
I've got a job.

PEGGY
(PEGGY puts the kettle down) A job? You? Yer, lazy layabout.

CECIL
That's not fair. I'm not lazy.

PEGGY
You certainly are around here.

CECIL
Admittedly, I'm not good at housework. But I do look after all your other needs, don't I?

PEGGY
(PEGGY smiles) Aye, that's true enough. You do at that. *(She kisses him)* You're a little darling when you want to be.

CECIL
I try my best.

PEGGY
Now tell me about this job. What sort of job is it?

CECIL
Would you believe it if I said it was an acting job?

PEGGY
What? Well, let's just say I can hardly believe it.

CECIL
And I start filming tomorrow.

PEGGY
Tomorrow?

CECIL
The actor playing my part got ill, and they needed someone to re-place him immediately.

PEGGY
So miracles do happen. In the last couple of months, you've been on so many auditions I've lost count.

CECIL
(CECIL ignores her remark) What was funny was that the casting director lined us up and got us to read. Then, looked at this ginger guy and told him he'd got the part, but then handed me the script. It turned out the casting director was cross-eyed.

PEGGY
(giggles) You mean, he was looking at apples and buying pears. So, is it a good part?

CECIL
Yes. I have six lines.

PEGGY
Well, that's an excellent start to your acting career.

CECIL
You'll never guess who I'll be working with.

PEGGY
Tell me it's someone I fancy.

CECIL
One, you will. James Mason.

PEGGY
I don't believe it.

CECIL
It's true. And Celia Johnson.

PEGGY
Oh, she's gorgeous. You must get their autographs for me.

CECIL
Just think. Tomorrow I will be brushing shoulders with film stars. Who knows, even hanging out with them.

PEGGY
(chuckles) Don't make me laugh. You'd have to be rich or famous too. Cecil, these people can be very cliquey, not to mention fickle.

CECIL
(CECIL gets angry) It's Peter, remember, call me Peter!

PEGGY
Okay, calm down. All I'm saying is those sorts only mix in their own circles.

CECIL
That's what Peter said.

PEGGY
Well, he was right. I just don't get it this obsession you have about mixing with celebrities. It's money you should be obsessed with. Then you'd be able to mix with who you like. Look, lad. There's nothing wrong with having big dreams as long as you're not too disappointed when they don't happen.

CECIL
But it will happen one day, I promise you.

PEGGY
Of course, it will pet. So I'd best darn your socks and iron your shirt for tomorrow. Now, what time do you have to be at the studio?

CECIL
Seven.

PEGGY
Then, I'd best set the alarm for five, and we can have a nice cuddle

and an early night. *(CECIL doesn't look thrilled at the prospect)*

LIGHTS FADE

ACT I SCENE VIII

NEXT DAY. EARLY EVENING LANDLADY'S FLAT.

PEGGY
(as CECIL enters, Peggy is sorting out washing) Hello love. How did it go?

CECIL
Okay.

PEGGY
So what was James Mason like?

CECIL
Never saw him.

PEGGY
Celia Johnson?

CECIL
Or her. My scene wasn't with either of them.

PEGGY
Oh, that's a shame. Who was it with then?

CECIL
Jonathan Charlesgud.

PEGGY
Didn't he get knighted?

CECIL
For services to the theatre.

PEGGY
I'm not too fond of all that business.

CECIL
Knighthoods?

PEGGY
That Shakespeare nonsense. I don't understand a word of it.

CECIL
He wouldn't even say good morning.

PEGGY
Snooty bugger, eh? So how did it go?

CECIL
It was fine in the run-through. But when the director shouted, 'Quiet on the set and then Action!' I went completely blank.

PEGGY
But why?

CECIL
It was in the silence and the sudden realisation the director, the crew,

the other actors, and even the tea lady were all staring at me, waiting for me to deliver my lines on cue.

PEGGY
So? That's what they pay you for.

CECIL
Yes, but I dried.

PEGGY
You did what?

CECIL
I just dried up. I forgot my lines. Then that high and mighty Sir Jonathan Charlesgud stepped in and told the director to cut my lines.

PEGGY
Bloody cheek.

CECIL
He said they were wasting valuable time. Before adding loudly, 'Obviously, he cannot act!' So the director agreed to cut four of my lines.

PEGGY
So you only had two left?

CECIL
I felt utterly humiliated. And if that wasn't bad enough, on my way home, it started raining, and who d'you think passes is his big fancy Rolls Royce?

PEGGY
James Mason?

CECIL
Sir Jonathan Charlesgud, no less. I thought he was going to offer me a lift because he slowed down.

PEGGY
That was nice of him.

CECIL
That's what I thought. But just as I got to the car, he leant forward and grinned. Wound up his window and sped off.

PEGGY
He sounds like a nasty piece of work. He'll get his comeuppance. What goes around comes around.

CECIL
I'll make sure of it.

PEGGY
Perhaps, you're not cut out for this acting lark. Some people can be great in the dressing room, yet once they are on stage. It's like their whole personality drains away with fright.

CECIL
Maybe, but until another audition comes up, I'll start looking for other work to get some money coming in.

PEGGY
What about extra work?

CECIL
That's what I just said, didn't I?

PEGGY
No, I mean working as a film extra, you know, between acting jobs.

CECIL
Film extra?

PEGGY
It just means you'll be doing what you've been doing, but with less responsibility. And as far as I understand it, film extras get good money.

CECIL
Really?

PEGGY
Or you could also work for one of those posh catering firms, serving drinks and fiddly bits on silver trays. That pays good money, too.

CECIL
That's also a good idea. But how can I get into this film extra work?

PEGGY
You'd have to join something called the Film Artists' Association.

CECIL
Which is what?

PEGGY
Their union.

CECIL
Oh no. I couldn't go through all that again.

PEGGY
No. It's easy to get one. Just pay a small fee, and bingo! You're in. It'll suit you. You'll be doing what you want most, mixing with famous actors. But without the worry of having to learn all those lines.

CECIL
Sounds good. But I like that catering idea too.

PEGGY
There's no reason you can't do both. You can do one when you're not doing the other. Just think, you'll be doing what you always wanted, mixing with the rich and famous.

CECIL
Yes, yes, I will be, won't I? Peggy, you are a star! *(CECIL embraces her)*

PEGGY
I'll leave the fantasies to you. *(CECIL embraces PEGGY)* What are you doing? Get off. You are insatiable. *(as they fall back onto the sofa, Peggy giggles)* Here we go again. You'll be the death of me.

LIGHTS FADE

END OF ACT I

ACT II. SCENE I

1950. FIVE YEARS LATER.
LANDLADY'S FLAT. DAYTIME.

PEGGY
(PEGGY is ironing while CECIL relaxes on the sofa) D'you need me
to iron that other white shirt for tonight?

CECIL
Yes, please. You know, Peggy, thanks to you. I've found something
I'm good at. I just love my work.

PEGGY
The catering or the extra work?

CECIL
The extra work especially. It's money for old rope, and you get fed.

PEGGY
You don't do so badly from the catering jobs either.

CECIL
You mean we don't do so badly. *(CECIL reaches into his pocket and
brings out a small string of pearls)* Turn around. *(CECIL Puts them
around PEGGY'S neck)* Now, let's look at you.

PEGGY
They are beautiful. Must be worth a fortune? Where did you get
them?

CECIL
The Duchess of Argyll's party last week. These people have so much. They don't know what they have. She won't miss them.

PEGGY
Last time, you stole her little diamond broach.

CECIL
No, that was from the Marchioness of Tewksbury's house.

PEGGY
Don't get me wrong. But I think you should stop while you're ahead. These are powerful people. You don't want them coming after you.

CECIL
Don't worry. I'm just one of many waiters. These people get so drunk they have no idea what's happening.

PEGGY
But they must suspect it's someone from the catering firm.

CECIL
It's not as if they will discover the loss right away. I always take things from the bottom, never the top of a drawer or jewel box. That way, there's less chance of it being missed immediately. Look at this beauty from last night. *(CECIL takes a cigarette from a gold cigarette case)* Sir Jonathan Charlesgud dropped it while ranting on about me not serving the drinks fast enough.

PEGGY
It was his party? But didn't he recognise you?

CECIL
(CECIL laughs) Of course not. They don't look at the waiter's face. Besides, it was payback for what he did.

PEGGY
But surely you have enough now? There's already quite a hoard, And what do we do with it all? I can't wear any of this in public.

CECIL
In a few years, when any interest in them has died down. We can sell them. Maybe retire. Who knows, even get married.

PEGGY
Are you serious? You'd marry me?

CECIL
Well, I don't see anyone else queuing up.

PEGGY
Cheeky bugger!

CECIL
I don't see why not. After all, we make a good team, don't we?

PEGGY
We do. But let me give it some thought. I don't want to jump into another marriage like last time.

CECIL
But we've been living together for nearly five years now.

PEGGY
Then a few more won't hurt then, will they?

BLACKOUT

ACT II. SCENE II

DAYTIME. LANDLADY'S LIVING ROOM. 1984.
The walls are covered with framed photographs of famous actors. The furniture and fittings are more up-to-date. PEGGY is lying on the sofa, covered in a blanket, watching the television.

PEGGY
(*PEGGY turns the sound down*) I'm not well, you know?

CECIL
Peggy, I do know. You tell me at least ten times a day. I don't want to hear about it anymore.

PEGGY
Just show a bit of sympathy now and again. That's all I ask.

CECIL
If I had the luxury of time, I would. But I'm too busy as it is.

PEGGY
Doing what? You're retired.

CECIL
Are you serious? When I'm not dealing with the tenants' problems. There's the cooking, washing, and shopping. Not to mention getting your prescriptions and sorting out your medicines.

PEGGY
It's not my fault I'm ill.

CECIL
True, but things were much easier when I was working.

PEGGY
I know, love, but you can't put the clock back. You had to give it up because of your allergies and your arthritis, remember?

CECIL
It was all that standing around that did it. I've got these pills, but they don't ease the pain.

PEGGY
(PEGGY is not listening as she's watching the television) Blimey, he's aged.

CECIL
Who?

PEGGY
Take a look.

CECIL
(CECIL looks over at the television) It's Jonathan Charlesgud. My god, he has aged. What's it about?

PEGGY
A place called Danton Manor. It's where all these famous old stars go to retire. All the big names, they all seem to live there.

CECIL
Really?

PEGGY
(PEGGY looks a CECIL and laughs) I know what you're thinking. Forget it. With the amount of acting work you've done. They
wouldn't let you through the door.

CECIL
Not that I'd want to, mind. But even if they begged me to move
there. I wouldn't. I'm over all that.

PEGGY
Come of it. You'd love it there. At last, being able to rub shoulders
with that lot.

CECIL
I've no idea what you're getting at.

PEGGY
Just look around this room. *(PEGGY gestures to the photos of famous faces on the walls)* You're obsessed with celebrities. You always have been.

CECIL
I'm not obsessed. Collecting signed photos is just a hobby.

PEGGY
Who d'you think you're fooling? If you ask me, you should have
seen a psychiatrist about it years ago. Oh, and by the way. If your
daft enough to believe that, after I've gone, they'd let you move into
Hardup Hall or whatever it's called. You'd be wasting your time.

CECIL
You mean Danton Manor.

PEGGY
See? You remembered the name fast enough.

CECIL
So what? And in any case, I don't see why they wouldn't let me in.

PEGGY
Because you'd need a lot more on your resume than a few bit parts and extra work, unless you were rich, that might help, so you'd best forget about it.

CECIL
All I was saying was it looked like an interesting programme.

PEGGY
Then you should watch more television instead of sitting there writing those silly fan letters. Then you might learn something. There are a lot of interesting things on the tele. There was a programme earlier about buying and selling property. It certainly cheered me up. Do you know what the houses are going for in this area?

CECIL
No idea. It's still a slum.

PEGGY
The best part of half a million quid.

CECIL
Your joking?

PEGGY
No, it's these yuppies moving in. They call it gentrification. That reminds me, I saw you on television this morning. In one of those Ivanhoe re-runs.

CECIL
With Roger Moore?

PEGGY
He's just finished filming another James Bond film. I think it'll be his last, though, he must be knocking on a bit by now.

CECIL
Was I on for long?

PEGGY
In Ivanhoe? Yes, at least two minutes. You were dressed up as a medieval soldier. I could only see your eyes, but you were still recognisable. Of course, you were so much younger then.

CECIL
It was over forty years ago. I remember that scene as if it were yesterday. It was with Roger and Sophia Loren. My line was...

PEGGY
Three cheers for Ivanhoe!

CECIL
That's right. Three cheers for Ivanhoe! I did that in just three takes.

PEGGY
For you, that was very good.

CECIL
Just hearing that line again gives me goose pimples.

PEGGY
It was lucky you kept that Equity ticket.

CECIL
Luck had little to do with it. To think, I once played opposite Roger Moore and Sophia Loren. And Larry...

PEGGY
Larry? Who's Larry?

CECIL
Olivier, of course.

PEGGY
Come off it. You were hardly on first-name terms with him or the others.

CECIL
What are you talking about?

PEGGY
And as for playing opposite them. You're not even in the same shot as the main actors. It's about time you owned up, if only to yourself.

CECIL
About what?

PEGGY
The fact you've never achieved what you really wanted in life.

CECIL
And what is that?

PEGGY
To be an actor, to become one of them. Part of their little circle.

CECIL
Don't be so daft.

PEGGY
It's you that's daft. Face it. You can't even act. If you ask me, you're completely bonkers! You should take all these photos down and get a life before it's too late.

CECIL
(CECIL disguises his anger with a smile) It's never too late.

PEGGY
Of course, it is.

CECIL
Not for us to get married, it isn't. *(CECIL puts his arms around her)* It's time I made a dishonest woman of you. *(CECIL grabs a rose from a vase and hands it to her)* So here goes. Peggy O'Brian, will you marry me?

PEGGY
Oh, go on with you.

CECIL
So is that a yes?

PEGGY
(PEGGY takes the rose) Well, I suppose a wedding would break the monotony of lying here watching television all day. *(they kiss)*

CECIL
Good, then I'll book the registry office.

LIGHTS FADE

ACT II. SCENE III

LANDLADY'S FLAT. EVENING A FEW WEEKS MONTHS. *PEGGY is lying on the sofa in the living room. There is a framed wedding photo on the side. CECIL is putting some pieces of jewellery into a small bag*

PEGGY
Where are you going with those?

CECIL
To that little jeweller, the one in Brighton. He's not too fussy about its history.

PEGGY
But why are you selling them now?

CECIL
Because after all this time. No one will be looking for them. And

they say there's going to be another recession next year.

PEGGY
I doubt I'll be around in 1985 to worry about it.

CECIL
We'd best be prepared with some hard cash. It's surprising how much of this stuff there is to shift.

PEGGY
I'm not surprised. You were petty pilfering those parties for years.

CECIL
Not so petty. Look at the size of these diamonds. *(CECIL hands her a broach)*

PEGGY
It's beautiful. *(disappointed)* They're much bigger my wedding ring. *(CECIL takes them back)* Can you change the channel for me?

CECIL
Of course, dear. *CECIL changes the channel on the television)* Okay, catch you later. I'm off. *(CECIL puts them in the bag and leaves)*

LIGHT FADE

ACT II. SCENE IV

THE LANDLADY'S LIVING ROOM. THE SAME EVENING.
PEGGY

(as CECIL enters, PEGGY is on the sofa writing) Hello love. How did it go? Did you get a reasonable price?

CECIL
Yes. He's very fair. I give him that. Five grand. *(CECIL shows her the cash)* When I cash in the rest, I reckon we'll have nearer a hundred and fifty.

PEGGY
And no questions?

CECIL
That's the beauty of it. Have you seen my inhaler? This pollution is getting worse. It's all those diesel fumes.

PEGGY
That's why my chest's so bad.

CECIL
(CECIL picks up his empty cigarette case) I think smoking all my cigarettes don't help.

PEGGY
There are times I can hardly breathe.

CECIL
(under his breath) There is some hope, then.

PEGGY
What d'you say?

CECIL
I said I'll put the kettle on.

PEGGY
That'll be lovely. I could do with a nice cuppa.

CECIL
(as CECIL goes to the kitchen, he notices Peggy is writing)
Who are you writing to?

PEGGY
Who am I going to write to? I've only my only cousin in Limerick,
and we haven't spoken since the wedding. I don't think she like you.

CECIL
What?

PEGGY
Us getting married.

CECIL
No that. *(CECIL points to her letter)*

PEGGY
If you really want to know. I'm writing my will before it's too late.

CECIL
(CECIL is surprised but manages to hide it) Good idea. *(jokingly)* I
hope you're not leaving it to a cat sanctuary. Or something stupid.

PEGGY
No, I've decided to leave the house to a donkey sanctuary in Spain.

CECIL
What?

PEGGY
I've seen it on television. They save badly abused donkeys. You should see the state they're in when they arrive. It would break your heart.

CECIL
It has already.

PEGGY
Don't worry. Nothing will change. You can keep my half of the sale of the jewellery and stay on here until your time comes.

CECIL
(CECIL uses his inhaler, takes a deep breath, and then hands her the tea) When you finish it. Sign it, and I'll witness it for you.

PEGGY
I'm glad you're not annoyed.

CECIL
Why would I be?

PEGGY
No reason, after all, I'm also leaving you all my savings.

CECIL
How much is that?

PEGGY
Quite a lot. Nearly fifteen thousand pounds. Of course, some will

have to go toward my funeral expenses.

CECIL
I'd better prep the dinner. I got you a nice bit of smoked haddock.

PEGGY
That's sweet of you.

CECIL
And I'll poach an egg and pop it on top, just as you like it.

PEGGY
You are spoiling me.

CECIL
And why not? We should celebrate.

PEGGY
Celebrate?

CECIL
Me selling some of the jewellery, and you writing your will. We've both achieved something today. I'll make it a special night and open that bottle of port from last Christmas.

PEGGY
Oh, but I mustn't. The doctor said no alcohol with my pills.

CECIL
Ah, don't listen to doctors. I'm on all kinds of pills. It doesn't stop me.

PEGGY
Maybe just a small one before dinner, then. *(CECIL opens the bottle and, pours some port into two very large wine glasses, and hands her one)* Oh, now that is a big glass. *(PEGGY chuckles)* What are you trying to do, kill me?

CECIL
(raises his glass) Now, would I do that?

PEGGY
(PEGGY chuckles) I'm only joking. Of course, you wouldn't. *(CECIL kisses her)*

LIGHTS FADE

ACT II. SCENE V

THE NEXT MORNING. LANDLADY'S LIVING ROOM
(the PEGGY is still on the sofa. CECIL removes her glasses, then takes the will and tears it up. He then replaces the large wine goblet with a small sherry glass and rings the doctor)

CECIL
Hello, doctor Grimshaw. This is Peggy O'Docherty's husband. I have some terrible news. I'm afraid my wife has passed on. I can't seem to wake her. Last night, she'd helped herself to a glass of port. I'm not a medical man, but I don't think she should have been drinking. You'll be right over? Okay, see you soon.

LIGHTS FADE

ACT II. SCENE VI

SAME MORNING. ONE HOUR LATER

DOCTOR GRIMSHAW
As I suspected. *(the doctor is by the sofa examining PEGGY with CECIL nervously looking on)*

CECIL
I feel bad going to bed early and leaving here alone. I could have prevented this.

DOCTOR GRIMSHAW
Come on now. I assume she told you? *(DOCTOR begins to write her death certificate)*

CECIL
Told me what?

DOCTOR GRIMSHAW
She had very little time left. Peggy had a weak heart. She had two or three weeks at most.

CECIL
With the amount she smoked, I'm not surprised.

DOCTOR GRIMSHAW
(seems confused at CECIL'S cold reaction) It didn't help. Here's her death certificate. *(DOCTOR hands CECIL the certificate)* I put down natural causes. I'll see myself out and leave you to make her funeral arrangements.

CECIL
Yes, I'll do that now. Thank you, doctor. *CECIL sees the doctor out and closes the door. Then he goes over to a drawer, brings out some brochures, looks at them and smiles. He picks up the phone and puts on his poshest accent)* Hello, is that Danton Manor? Can I speak to Mrs Mappleforth? Yes, I'll wait. Hello Mrs Mappleforth? This is Peter Brock. We talked before about my moving into your establishment. Well, I'm now in a financial position to go ahead.

LIGHTS FADE

ACT II. SCENE. VII

DAYTIME - DANTON MANOR - SIX MONTHS LATER - PRESENT DAY. 1985.

DAME SYBIL
(DAME SYBIL looks over at CECIL, who is still at the bar chatting to SIR JOHN, who then storms off) Oh dear, it seems Sir John has stormed off and left Mr Brock on his own. It's the perfect time to invite him over and see what skeletons we can rattle out of his closet.

EDITH
Good, then, as a Dame of the British Empire. Why don't you give him one of your royal waves?

DAME SYBIL
Very droll. I think you're jealous. An OBE isn't quite the same, is it, dear?

EDITH
True. Unless I wear it, nobody knows I have a gong. *(DAME SYBIL gently waves at CECIL, who smiles and walks over to their table with more champagne)*

CECIL
Ladies, all I can say is. You're both far more beautiful the closer one gets.

EDITH
I do hope that's not all you can say. Otherwise, it'll be a one-way conversation.

CECIL
(chuckles) Honestly, it's true! Let me introduce myself. I'm Peter Brock.

EDITH
And I'm Edith, and this is Dame Sybil.

CECIL
Yes, I know. Your reputations precede you.

DAME SYBIL
In that case, I can only say I hope our reputations are intact. With all the gossip that goes on around here, you never quite know.

CECIL
I may have only been here a short time, but I do get your point.

DAME SYBIL
That's why we like to keep ourselves to ourselves.

CECIL
(CECIL pours more champagne and raises his glass) Then here's to new friends.

DAME SYBIL
To friendships old and new.

EDITH
I see you're already friends with some of the other residents.

CECIL
A few.

DAME SYBIL
From what we've seen, you've got a veritable fan club.

CECIL
Well, I've met some of them before, at different parties. But that was years ago.

DAME SYBIL
Then it's possible you were at some of my soirees.

EDITH
And mine.

CECIL
Yes, it is. Didn't you use to have your parties catered for?

DAME SYBIL
We both did.

CECIL
That's right. I remember they were huge affairs. Anyone who was anyone was there.

EDITH
That's true. So you must have been at them.

CECIL
That's where I met you. It was just chit-chat about the canapes and drinks needing to be served faster.

EDITH
I'm so sorry, but those waiters could be so lazy.

CECIL
I can understand. I've experienced that myself.

DAME SYBIL
You appear to have been arguing with Sir John. What was it about?

CECIL
No, Not at all.

DAME SYBIL
But you were tugging on his jacket.

CECIL
I was just fooling with him. Old Johnnie hangs around like an unwanted puppy dog, waiting to be thrown a bone.

DAME SYBIL
More like a double whiskey in his case. Your bar bill must be a small fortune.

CECIL
(CECIL smiles) Don't worry. I can afford it.

DAME SYBIL
I'm relieved to hear it.

CECIL
Who is that man sitting at that table in the corner?

EDITH
Do you mean Roy Dean? Surely you recognise him. You know from films like We Need the Stars. Not the Moon and Flight of Fancy.

CECIL
It's not him, is it?

DAME SYBIL
Granted, he's aged a bit, but yes, it is.

CECIL
Wow, I'm a huge fan.

EDITH
I wouldn't use that term around here, dear. People's egos are big enough as it is.

DAME SYBIL
True, but Roy Dean isn't like that. Quite the opposite, considering he's also a war hero.

CECIL
Was he, indeed?

EDITH
He was a pilot in the RAF. But he signed up under another name. So nobody would know who he was.

DAME SYBIL
Didn't he spend most of his time defending Malta?

EDITH
Something like that. He was decorated for it.

CECIL
I'd like to meet him. Maybe I should introduce myself.

DAME SYBIL
No, I wouldn't do that if I were you. He likes to keep his own company.

EDITH
Although very occasionally, he gives a little dinner party in his suite. We went to one, remember?

DAME SYBIL
That was over a year ago. Peter, if, in the unlikely event, you ever get an invite to one of these rare occasions. You should go. You'll find him rather interesting. *(at that moment, a waiter comes over and hands CECIL a note)*

CECIL
(CECIL seems surprised) Talk of the devil.

DAME SYBIL
What is it?

CECIL
Mr Dean has invited me over to his table for a drink.

EDITH
That's quite an honour in itself. Who knows, one of his dinners could be on the horizon.

CECIL
Do forgive me, ladies, but I had better go over there before he chang es his mind.

DAME SYBIL
Yes, you had. And remember. Tell us everything that happened.
(CECIL leaves the champagne and walks over to ROY DEAN)

ROY
Do sit down. It's Peter Brock, isn't it?

CECIL
It is, yes.

ROY
Delighted to meet you. I'm Roy Dean. Now, what can I get you to drink?

CECIL
I know who you are. And it would give me great pleasure to buy you one.

ROY
Sorry, my round, old boy. So what will it be? *(the waiter arrives)*

CECIL
I'll have whatever you're having.

ROY
Two whiskies it is, then. *(ROY looks at the waiter)* Make those doubles

CECIL
I won't argue with that. *(CECIL brings out his nasal spray and squirts it up his nose)*

ROY
What's that thing for?

CECIL
It's just a spray to clear my sinuses.

ROY
Why, what's wrong with them?

CECIL
Oh, it's nothing too serious. It's just an antihistamine. I do have pills that are more effective, but the spray is easier. Mind you. if I use too much, it's not good for my asthma.

ROY
Interesting.

CECIL
Is it?

ROY
I noticed you were using it earlier. I was curious, that's all.

(their drinks arrive) Well, here's to... What did you call them?

CECIL
Allergies.

ROY
To allergies, cheers. And that reminds me. I'm due at my doctor's. D'you have the time?

CECIL
(looks at his watch) Coming up to five.

ROY
That's a lovely watch. May I see it?

CECIL
Yes, of course. *(CECIL takes it off his wrist and hands it to ROY, who then examines it)*

ROY
As I thought, an Omega CK2129? So you were in the RAF? Good man. Me too.

CECIL
(nervously) No, it was my father's.

ROY
He was a pilot. I take it. *(ROY hands him back the watch. CECIL seems nervous)* Was he one of the few?

CECIL
Sorry? Few what?

ROY
Battle of Britain and all that.

CECIL
Oh, I'm not sure. I hardly ever saw him.

ROY
For my own sins, I was stuck out in Malta, stopping the Gerries from getting a toehold in North Africa.

CECIL
It must have been rough.

ROY
It was. Forgive me. But I have to dash off to my doctor.

CECIL
Nothing serious, I hope?

ROY
No, just insomnia. I've run out of sleeping pills. And I don't want to be late. My doctor can be a bit tetchy if I am.

CECIL
(CECIL looks disappointed) Oh, okay. Well, it's been nice chatting.

ROY
If you've nothing planned, how about joining me for dinner at my place tonight? We can continue our chat then. And I promise you one thing, the food will be good. Do you like puddings?

CECIL
Puddings?

ROY
You know. Things like trifle, gateau, and the like.

CECIL
I have to confess...

ROY
Please, I'd be more than happy if you did.

CECIL
I have a weakness for anything sweet.

ROY
Excellent. Then we must see what I can tickle your palate with.

CECIL
Now that does sound tempting. What time?

ROY
Say, six o'clock for drinks.

BLACKOUT

ACT II SCENE VIII

SAME EVENING, ROY DEAN'S APARTMENT
ROY is busy setting the table when there is a knock on the door. He goes over and opens it. *CECIL is standing at the entrance clutching a bottle of champagne)*

ROY
Right on time. Oh, and how kind, champagne, no less? I was going to tempt you to an aperitif. But if you prefer this stuff?

CECIL
An aperitif sounds good. We can have both. At least, if I get a bit tiddly, I don't have far to go.

ROY
True, you're on the first floor, aren't you?

CECIL
Yes, my rooms are right above you.

ROY
I prefer this floor, I can get into the garden, without having to trapes through reception. Now, how about a large dubonnet? It'll get your appetite going.

CECIL
I've never had one before.

ROY
It's just fortified wine mixed with herbs, quinine, and lord knows what. Trust the French. They know what they are doing when it comes to eating and drinking. *(ROY hands CECIL a dubonnet)*

CECIL
Lovely, thank you

ROY
Come and sit yourself down at the table. And I'll serve the appetiser. It's just a cantaloupe melon to clean the palate.

CECIL
(CECIL sips his drink) This is very nice. But I can taste that quinine.

ROY
(Roy laughs) Well, that's not such a bad thing. We can't have you catching malaria.

CECIL
That's true. *(CECIL looks at the table settings)* Am I the only one coming?

ROY
I'm afraid so. I hope you don't mind.

CECIL
No, not at all. I'm flattered.

ROY
I thought it would give us a chance to get to know each other better.

CECIL
Good idea. As there are so many questions, I want to ask you, especially about your film career.

ROY
Ah, there's plenty of time for all that. Now a little top-up?

CECIL
Yes, thanks. I must say this melon is so sweet. It just slips down.

ROY
That's what I was hoping. Are you ready for the next course?
I don't want to rush you. But there are lots more lovely goodies to

get through yet. *(ROY takes away CECIL'S plate and replaces it with a variety of cold cuts and a large bowl of mixed salad)*

CECIL
This isn't a dinner. It's a banquet.

ROY
I thought you'd want something other than hot food on a warm evening like this. So dig in while I serve the wine. *(ROY goes over to a side table. And with his back to CECIL, he opens a bottle of wine, pours some into his own glass and the remainder into a decanter. ROY goes back to the table and fills CECIL'S empty glass)*

CECIL
Thank you.

ROY
It's an Italian Barolo, one of my favourites. Full-bodied and got a kick to it.

CECIL
(CECIL takes a sip) It's perfect.

ROY
So tell me, Peter. I hope you don't mind if I call you Peter.

CECIL
No, not at all. There's no reason to be formal.

ROY
No, quite. I must say, Peter Brock. It's a good name for an actor.

CECIL
A friend once said it just rolls off the tongue and sounds as English as a game of cricket.

ROY
I have to admit it certainly does sound very English. *(ROY chuckles)* And as a stage name, it's almost better than mine. But I'm sure I know that name from somewhere. *(ROY gets up and pours CECIL more wine)* Perhaps I've seen you in something.

CECIL
It's possible. But then, I've had a very modest career compared to you.

ROY
there is no reason for modesty around here. I happen to know you're a fine actor.

CECIL
But how would you know?

ROY
Just call me psychic. *(ROY laughs)* No, it's just that I have a gut feeling about you.

CECIL
I might have to pinch myself.

ROY
Oh, dear, not another allergy?

CECIL
Nothing like that. It's just I can't believe I'm sitting here.

ROY
I can only say I'm delighted to say you are.

CECIL
But being served dinner by the famous Roy Dean.

ROY
Enough of all that nonsense. After all, we are all actors here.
(ROY raises his glass and looks at CECIL) Granted, some are better at acting than others. *(ROY gets up to remove CECIL'S plate)* Splendid. You must have enjoyed that.

CECIL
Yes, thank you. I did.

ROY
I hope you still have room for pudding. As I've made a special effort just for you. *(ROY points to the desserts)*

CECIL
I certainly do. They look scrumptious.

ROY
Which one would you prefer? Strawberry cheesecake or black Forest gateau with lashings of cream?

CECIL
It's a difficult decision.

ROY
Then I insist you try both. Eat as much as you can manage, as they will only be thrown away.

CECIL
Why?

ROY
For me, it would be like eating poison.

CECIL
But you said you also liked puddings. You may have an allergy to sucrose or a chemical in the sugar.

ROY
All I know is that I'd be as sick as a dog if I took just one bite.

CECIL
Poor you. I'm so sorry.

ROY
Please don't be. I promise you. I'm getting far more enjoyment seeing you tucking into them.

CECIL
(CECIL smiles) Then I'll have to do them justice. After all, it would be a terrible waste.

ROY
That's what I was hoping you were going to say.

CECIL
You can't believe how much this means to me. You treating me like I'm a friend.

ROY
I'm sure you know what they say about keeping friends close and

your...

CECIL
Sorry, what did you say? *(CECIL begins to feel the effects of the wine. His accent slips back to a slight Irish brogue)*

ROY
Goodness me. Was that an Irish accent I just heard?

CECIL
I was originally from Ireland. But I lost my accent a long time ago.

ROY
Yes, but not quite, it seems. Now come on, eat up.

CECIL
I'm doing my best.

ROY
There it goes again.

CECIL
What?

ROY
Your accent. How can I put it? It slipped.

CECIL
Yes, I'm afraid it happens when I'm tired.

ROY
Don't worry. Mine slips, too, sometimes.

CECIL
Yours? But you have a beautiful speaking voice.

ROY
Ah, no, I'm afraid it's as phoney as yours. *(ROY pours CECIL more wine)*

CECIL
(laughs) Phoney? I hope that wasn't meant as an insult.

ROY
Not at all. I also had elocution lessons.

CECIL
I worked very hard to lose my accent.

ROY
(ROY gets up and pours CECIL some Armagnac) And you almost succeeded. Now try this. It's a Baron de Lustrac Armagnac 1945. I have yet to try it myself. I bought it the year my son died. I decided to save it for a special occasion. *(ROY pours CECIL a glass)*

CECIL
I'm honoured. But why is this a special occasion?

ROY
I'll explain later. Just have a sniff. It has such an elegant nose on it. You get a wonderful aroma of orange blossom.

CECIL
You're right, it does, but I'm still getting that aftertaste from the dubonnet. What did you mean by it when you said I almost succeeded?

ROY
It was when your accent slipped. You could say it was the final nail in your coffin. And that's what makes this such a special occasion.

CECIL
What are you talking about?

ROY
Oh, didn't I say? Murder.

CECIL
Murder. What murder?

ROY
My son.

CECIL
Your son was murdered? I'm so sorry.

ROY
I'm glad to hear you say that. Mr O'Docherty.

CECIL
I prefer my stage name, Brock.

ROY
But it's not your stage name, is it?

CECIL
Of course, it is. I can show you my Equity card.

ROY
Come now, what you mean is you can show me Peter's Equity card.

CECIL
I'm sorry you've lost me.

ROY
Your real name isn't Peter Brock. It's Cecil O'Docherty. And in 1945, you rented a room in Pimlico at Peggy O'Brian's boarding house.

CECIL
What of it?

ROY
The same boarding house where my son was gassed.

CECIL
That's right, Peter was drunk and forgot to light the fire.

ROY
True, the coroner's report did claim that Peter had died due to carbon monoxide poisoning.

CECIL
of course, that's what killed him.

ROY
No, that's what the inquest said. What puzzled me was that his stomach contained not only a large amount of alcohol but also a high amount of an antihistamine. A combination that, at the very least, would make a person extremely drowsy. Maybe pass out, or even worse.

CECIL
But the coroner said it was death by misadventure.

ROY
Yes, odd that. Considering Peter never drank, and as far as I know, unlike yourself, he didn't have any allergies to merit taking antihistamines.

CECIL
With family living away, you never quite know, do you?

ROY
Oh, I think I do. Well, I certainly do now.

CECIL
I'm sorry. I don't understand.

ROY
I feel guilty.

CECIL
Why would you?

ROY
After my wife died, I became so consumed with self-pity. Instead of being there for him, I sent Peter to the country to live with his aunt and immersed myself in my work.

CECIL
That's a sad story. But what has that got to do with me?

ROY
I'll come to that.

CECIL
Up till now, it's been a lovely evening. But I think it's time I left. *(CECIL coughs)* My asthma is starting to play up.

ROY
Please, don't rush off on my account. I'm just getting to the interesting part.

CECIL
Really? I wish you would.

ROY
With me based in Malta, it was only when I was on short breaks back in England, working on films for the government, that I actually got a chance to see Peter. Even so...

CECIL
Just get to the point.

ROY
The point is. We always stayed in contact. Sometimes by phone but usually by mail. Peter would tell me what he was up to, especially about a friendship that had developed with a certain Cecil O'Docherty.

CECIL
We weren't exactly friends. We never socialised. We just had a chat occasionally. And was only if I happened bumped into him.

ROY
Now, that does surprise me. In one of his letters, Peter says that he had been giving you elocution lessons. And that you'd been practically living together. What's more he had grown fond of you. I always suspected he had, how should I put it, a more sensitive side to him. But that was his business. After all, he was twenty-one.

CECIL
What are you getting at?

131

ROY
You, murdering my son.

CECIL
Are you mad?

ROY
Not Mad. Just angry. Angry that I don't have the physical strength to strike you so hard you'd never get up again. Because I know you killed him.

CECIL
If I were you. I wouldn't say another word. That's slander right there.

ROY
I think a judge might disagree when I show him the evidence.

CECIL
What evidence? Don't make me laugh.

ROY
That watch on your wrist for a start. It's Peter's watch. It has an inscription on the back.

CECIL
There is no inscription.

ROY
Open the back of the watch.

CECIL
(CECIL opens the back of the watch) I can't read it. It's just gibberish.

ROY
Not quite. It's Polish. It says. Happy 21st birthday, Piotr, my darling son. From your loving father. He would never have parted with it.

CECIL
Well, he did, didn't he? He gave it to me. So what?

ROY
But you said you hardly spoke to him? So why would he have given it to you? Admit it. You stole it.

CECIL
I was only trying to help, that's all. Look, I don't feel right. Can you get me some water? *(ROY goes to the kitchen area and brings CECIL a glass of water. As CECIL reaches for it, ROY refuses to give it to him)*

ROY
After you tell me how you got the watch. Or perhaps you'd prefer to tell the police instead?

CECIL
Don't be such a daft old fool. You don't really believe the police would still be interested. It must be forty years ago.

ROY
In that case, you have nothing to worry about. So why not, for this old fool's sake, just tell the truth!

CECIL
(CECIL coughs, then gets angry and bangs his fist on the table) Just give me that water!

ROY

Or what? If I were you. I'd calm down, old darling. After all, You're getting a little old for that act. *(ROY hands CECIL the glass. CECIL gulps down the water and hands it back to ROY)*

CECIL

You've got it all wrong. I was the hero of the hour. I broke the door down and opened the windows to try and save him.

ROY

And that's when you took the watch?

CECIL

He didn't need it anymore.

ROY

But the landlady said it was her who broke the door down. Why would she say that?

CECIL

Oh, well, you might as well know. It was all so long ago. It was because Peggy said she didn't want to involve me in a scandal.

ROY

What is that supposed to mean?

CECIL

Get me some more water, will you?

ROY

It's coming. You said scandal. *(Roy goes over to the kitchen area, brings some water, and hands it to him)* What scandal?

CECIL
As you said, your son was sensitive. Face it. He was a Nancy boy.

ROY
That's a nasty way of putting it. So, I take it you would have been the other half of this scandal? Then, surely that makes you homosexual.

CECIL
Even if I were, and I'm not. It still wouldn't make me a murderer.

ROY
Maybe not. But coupled with the fact you stole Peter's Equity card and his identity.

CECIL
What makes you think I did?

ROY
I recognised the name Peter Brock the moment you arrived here. It was going to be Peter's professional stage name. There was mention of it in one of his letters. He told me that he'd registered it with the actors union. And as Equity will not allow the same name to be registered twice. That means you are using his card.

CECIL
Is that a fact?

ROY
It is. But what I still cannot fathom, is what parts you played as an actor. I've never seen Peter Brock's name on any credits. Your acting parts must have been so small you didn't get any. And that's why you fell under my radar. Until you arrived here, that is.

CECIL
I'm feeling terrible. I've definitely overeaten. It's time for my bed.
But before I go, *(sarcastically)* I should compliment you on a fine
dinner and the free entertainment thrown in. I found it most amusing.

ROY
You're welcome.

CECIL
You really should write a novel. *(CECIL tries to stand up but falls
back into his chair)* I must be more pissed than I thought.

ROY
I'm pleased you found this evening entertaining. But, of course, unlike a novel, it's not fiction.

CECIL
But it is circumstantial.

ROY
You're right. It is.

CECIL
I've had enough of this. I'm tired. I'm going to bed. *(CECIL again
attempts to up)* I can't get out of this chair. Help me up.

ROY
Of course. *(ROY goes towards CECIL)* After you admit to killing
my son.

CECIL
This conversation has become very repetitive. You're being ex-
tremely overdramatic. You should do less talking and more writing.
You'd have that novel written in no time.

ROY
I might just do that, once I know how this evening pans out. So go on, do me a favour, just admit it, and I'll have my ending.

CECIL
Just listen to yourself. Are you seriously asking me to admit to kill ing your son? *(laughs)* Over my dead body.

ROY
Then, I'm afraid. It just might have to come to that.

CECIL
Oh? Is that a threat?

ROY
Yes. You must be feeling the side effects by now.

CECIL
What side effects?

ROY
Of your meal. To be fair. You did say you felt unwell, and you've been coughing and wheezing a lot.

CECIL
That's just my asthma playing up.

ROY
I don't think it's your asthma. And unless I'm wrong, which I'm sure I'm not. If I don't call an ambulance soon, it will only get worse.

CECIL
(CECIL tries again to get out of the chair but in vain) You crazy, old fool. What have you done? *(CECIL looks down at his empty plate)*

Don't tell me you've poisoned the food?

ROY
I'm afraid I had little choice. As you can see, I don't have a gas fire, so carbon monoxide poisoning wasn't an option. *(ROY pours CECIL some more Armagnac)* But don't worry. I'm sure you'll be pleased to know this fine Armagnac isn't poisoned. That would have been a terrible waste. It's far too good to spoil. But, I have to admit everything else is, especially the puddings.

CECIL
The puddings. Why them especially?

ROY
You have a sweet tooth.

CECIL
(surprised) True, I do have a sweet tooth. But how did you know?

ROY
You can thank Peter for that. It seems you had a penchant for his aunt Daisy's cakes, which was lucky for me, as all that sugar made it easier to disguise the bitter aftertaste of the poison.

CECIL
Poison? But you said that was the quinine in the Dubonett.

ROY
Cinchona, one of the herbs, it contains quinine. I had to say something, in case you became suspicious. In fact it was probably the antihistamine. You did say too much of it is bad for your asthma.

CECIL
Antihistamine? *(smirks)* Then, it's not all bad news. Even with the

alcohol, that's hardly going to kill me.

ROY
Normally, I'd agree. But to ensure it will, I took the liberty of substituting my sleeping pills to compensate for the lack of gas in this room.

CECIL
lack of gas? What are you on about? I've had enough of this nonsense. Just help me get me back to my room.

ROY
There's no point. Because if I don't dial 999 soon, you will undoubtedly die.

CECIL
You're serious!

ROY
Deadly.

CECIL
Then, for god's sake, ring for an amulance.

ROY
(ROY takes CECIL'S arm and looks at his watch) If the time on Peter's watch is correct. By my reckoning, you have about another twenty minutes before you pass out. Then it'll be only a matter of time before you slip into a coma.

CECIL
Please, just stop this madness and just call for an ambulance.

ROY
I will. The moment you tell me the truth. So I'll ask you again. Did you kill my son? A simple yes or no.

CECIL
It wasn't as simple as that.

ROY
Oh, should I take that as a yes? Was it a yes?

CECIL
(CECIL grimaces) My stomach!

ROY
Was that a yes? Look, if I don't ring them soon, you're going to die.

CECIL
For pity's sake.

ROY
If that's what you're after. Then I'm afraid you're out of luck. All my pity is reserved for the day you met my son.

CECIL
Oh, come on... Try and see it from my side.

ROY
Are you insane? How stupid of me, of course, you are.

CECIL
I only wanted to be famous... *(CECIL looks around the back at ROY* And this, of course.

ROY
This?

CECIL
You know, being friends with and being respected by people like you.

ROY
You poor deluded creature. I'm not your friend.*((laughs)* Respect you? I detest you. You're a killer. You killed my son!

CECIL
But don't you see? I had no choice. Without that equity card, all this could never have happened. I'm sorry, but it was the only way. You, as an actor, can understand that, surely? Ouch! *(grips his stomach)* This is getting painful.

ROY
Yes, I'm afraid those little cramps will only get worse. But then, with what you've eaten, *ROY smiles)* I'm hardly surprised. So, I can take it. You're admitting you did kill Peter?

CECIL
I mean, it's really painful... Now come on, you've got to help me.

ROY
I will, once you've answered my question.

CECIL
(CECIL grips his stomach) Okay, I admit it. ROY
You admit it. Admit what exactly? Just say it!

CECIL
Say what?

ROY
I want to hear you say. I killed Peter!

CECIL
Okay! I killed him. Satisfied? Now ring for the bloody ambulance!

ROY
No.

CECIL
What? So you are going to kill me?

ROY
As tempting as it was. I only put two of my sleeping pills in that concoction, not enough to kill you, just enough to relax you. They are far too strong. Any more mixed with the alcohol would have proven fatal.

CECIL
But why?

ROY
To make you more susceptible to telling the truth.

CECIL
Are you saying I don't need an ambulance?

ROY
Bicarbonate of soda would be more helpful.

CECIL
What? Are you serious?

ROY
I'm afraid so. I'll get you some. *(ROY puts some bicarbonate of soda in a glass of water)*

CECIL
Hold on, so this dinner wasn't poisoned?

ROY
No. I suppose it wasn't

CECIL
So all this plying me with drink and god knows what else was just an elaborate charade to get me to talk?

ROY
You have to admit it worked. *(ROY hands him the glass)*

CECIL
You even convinced me you were my friend.

ROY
(laughs) I must say, as an actor, that was the most challenging role I've ever had to play. Considering how much I loathe you.

CECIL
And to think I believed you. What a joke.

ROY
It wasn't meant to be funny. But it did the trick. You finally told me what I needed to know.

CECIL
Rubbish! I'm drunk. And you've drugged me, telling me I was dying. So, I can hardly be held accountable for what I say.

143

ROY
But I promise you, you will be.

CECIL
Right, that's it. I've had enough. I'm leaving.

ROY
So soon? I was just getting started.

CECIL
(Cecil smirks) Oh, and by the way, do feel free to go to the police. After all, it'll only be your word against mine. And, whatever you think you have on me, is at best, no more than circumstantial.

ROY
True. But then, to paraphrase a poor cat. There are more than ways to skin a rat.

CECIL
Please, no more speeches. Just help me back to my room, and we'll say no more about it.

ROY
(ROY Begins to help CECIL out of the chair) But of course, you won't be able to avoid the scandal.

CECIL
What scandal?

ROY
The one I will create tomorrow when I tell the other residents of this fine establishment that you're not only an imposter but a murderer.

CECIL
(laughs) They'll never believe you. You forget how popular I am. Remember, everybody here likes me. They need me...

ROY
For free drinks. Nothing more. Poor Cecil, you forget they are actors. When it comes to sincerity, they are on a par with politicians kissing babies.

CECIL
Either way, you'd be wasting your time. And your Peter's watch won't prove a thing.

ROY
We shall just have to see. As first thing in the morning, I intend to ring the Actors Union regarding Peter's membership. Which, I'm sure, will warrant an investigation of some kind for illegal possession. But that's not the worst of it.

CECIL
So what is?

ROY
The real fireworks begin when Equity cancels your membership. Which in turn will take away your eligibility to live here at Danton Manor. You'll be homeless.

CECIL
You wouldn't do that?

ROY
Happily! And when the other residents hear the story, it'll not only give them enough gossip to keep them going for years. You'll be entirely ostracised. You'll not only have nowhere to live but no friends

either. No matter how many free drinks you offer them.

CECIL

You're bluffing. And in any case, what good will any of this to do?

ROY

You mean, seeing you driven out of here and your murderous, duplicitous life finally exposed? It won't bring Peter back. But I'm sure I'll sleep much better for it. And I won't be dependent on these anymore. *(ROY takes a box of sleeping pills out of his pocket)*

CECIL

You do realise you're giving me little choice but to...

ROY

Do the right thing. Think about it. What's the alternative? By this time tomorrow. You will have been arrested on suspicion of murder. But that's not the best of it. The best of it is when I go to the press. Then you'll, at last, get what you really wanted.

CECIL

What I really wanted?

ROY

Yes. Something you've always craved for.

CECIL

Which is what exactly?

ROY

Fame... You'll be famous. I wouldn't be surprised if you made the front page of every newspaper in this country.

CECIL
Really? Do you think so?

ROY
Yes, but for all the wrong reasons. You'll be despised and hated. What's more...

CECIL
That's enough!

ROY
Of course, there is a way you can avoid all that.

CECIL
How?

ROY
As I say, by doing the right thing. The decent thing.

CECIL
What you really mean is I should finish the job for you.

ROY
Now that would be entirely your decision. But if it were me. I'd quit while I was still ahead... Bow out, so to speak. Leaving my public wanting more. After all, nobody needs to know the truth.

CECIL
But you'd be first to tell them.

ROY
Why would I?

CECIL
Why wouldn't you? What would stop you?

ROY
Peace of mind...

CECIL
What's that supposed to mean?

ROY
Isn't it obvious?

CECIL
No, it's not. I don't get it.

ROY
If, as you put it. You did finish the job for me, in other words. Kill yourself. As far as Peter goes, justice would have been served. And at last, I can put this whole wretched business behind me. So what would be the point of torturing myself by raking it all up again?

CECIL
Hmm. I suppose...

ROY
And think about this. Instead of a scandal and the horrors of prison, you'll have a grand send-off, with all your celebrity friends in attendance paying their respects and singing your praises, quite literally.

CECIL
D'you think?

ROY
Of course! They'll all be there at the graveside. I'll make sure of it.

Just imagine it. For once in your life... *(ROY coughs)* Death. You'll be the star attraction.

CECIL
Yes, yes. I would be, wouldn't I?

ROY
I'll also get you an obituary in The Stage. The actor's newspaper. Now, what could be grander than that?

CECIL
Seriously?

ROY
I promise you. I'll write it myself.

CECIL
That really would be something if you wrote it. And, as you say, it would avoid all the unpleasantness.

ROY
Not forgetting, a very long prison sentence.

CECIL
There is that, of course.

ROY
I can't imagine what it must be like being locked up in a cell with other convicted murderers. Can you?Or worse. Serial killers. You know, if you think about it...

CECIL
I don't want to think about it.

ROY

You know, you really would be lucky to survive prison. If it were me, I know what I'd choose.

CECIL

But it's not you is it? But when you put it like that, the alternative does seem to make sense.

ROY

Of course, it does. Come on, you know it does.

CECIL

(CECIL takes a deep breath) Perhaps. Either way. I promise I'll give it some serious thought before making a decision. I'll let you know in the morning. By then, I'll have a clear head and be able to think straight.

ROY

I'm afraid by then you won't have a decision to make.

CECIL

Why not?

ROY

By morning, this place will be crawling with police.

CECIL

Not if you don't call them.

ROY

But by then, I would have.

CECIL
Oh, come on, you can wait just few more hours, surely?

ROY
I'm afraid not. I've waited far too long as it is. *(ROY picks up the phone and slowly dials three digits. As it rings, CECIL goes over and takes the phone from ROY'S hand and replaces the receiver)*

CECIL
There has to be another way to settle this... I know, what if?

ROY
What if what?

CECIL
Now, don't get angry.

ROY
Why would I?

CECIL
What if we come to some sort of arrangement? After all, I have plenty of money.

ROY
What's money got to do with anything?

CECIL
(scoffs) Oh, come off it! When did you last make a film? It must be at least twenty years ago.

ROY
So?

151

CECIL
So, like most of the others in here. I'm sure you also would be grateful for a little extra cash...

ROY
You bastard! I'm warning you. Not another word! *(ROY picks up a knife and points it at CECIL.)* Damn it. Now look what you've made me do. You've made me lose my temper. Something I promised myself I wouldn't do.

CECIL
(nervous) Okay. There's no need for violence. So calm down. Come on, you said you wouldn't get angry.

ROY
Then, for your own sake, don't make me angrier than I already am. Because if you persist in adding insult to injury by trying to bribe me. I'll not only get angry, but I'll get angry to the point I'd be willing to go to prison for you.

CECIL
Your joking?

ROY
Do I look like I'm joking? *(ROY is still pointing the knife at CECIL)*.

CECIL
(looks nervously at the knife) No, I don't believe you are. You would, wouldn't you?

ROY
Only if I have to.

CECIL
In that case, put the knife down.

ROY
I will, once you make up your mind.

CECIL
Come on, you can't be serious about using that?

ROY
Deadly.

CECIL
Then it seems I'm running out of options.

ROY
No, you still have two.

CECIL
You mean prison or suicide? That's not much of a choice, is it?

ROY
Don't see it like that. See it as a choice between shame or fame.

CECIL
Prison being shameful, I get that. But suicide?

ROY
Why even use that word? Don't be so negative. Try to be more positive and see it as an easier, more dignified way out of your predicament, with your phoney name and reputation still intact. And what's more, it's painless.

CECIL
There has to be another option., surely? *(CECIL starts snivelling)*

ROY
There is. *(ROY gently waves the knife)* But that would be painful. No, I'm sorry, old darling, I'm afraid there isn't. And, what's more, if you attempt to delay the inevitable any longer, you won't have any if you attempt to delay the inevitable any longer, you won't have any options. I'll decide for you. So, stop snivelling. For once in your life, behave like a gentleman. Pull yourself together and decide your fate, cool, calm and collectively.

CECIL
(CECIL slowly pulls himself together) In that case, as a gentleman, if it's not too much trouble. I'll ask you for a doggy bag.

ROY
A doggy bag?

CECIL
If you don't mind, I'll take the rest of this Black Forest gateau with me. It may not be good for my health, but I have to admit it is delicious.

ROY
Yes, I'm sure it is. *(ROY grins as he places the gateau into a bag. He then helps CECIL stand up)*

CECIL
Oh, and while I'm at it, may I ask another little favour?

ROY
Of course, ask away.

CECIL

Could I also take the remains of the Armagnac 45?

ROY

With pleasure. For me, 1945 was a horrible year.

CECIL

And as you won't be needing them anymore, I'm sure you won't mind if I take the rest of your sleeping pills.

ROY

I'd be delighted if you did. *(ROY opens a drawer, brings out another bottle of sleeping pills and rattles the bottle)* Ah! A full bottle! Make sure you take these as well. *(He puts them in the bag).* They are bound to do the trick. I'd swear by them. Just one is enough to knock me out.

CECIL

(*sarcastically*) That's very generous of you.

ROY

Oh, please. Don't give it another thought.

CECIL

(as ROY makes up the doggy bag. CECIL pours some more wine and gulps it down) Oh, and by the way. Before I forget, would you apologise to the others for me? As I don't think I'll be down for breakfast... or dinner, come to that.

ROY
It'll be my pleasure. It will save me from having to make that call in the morning. Now, the least I can do is help you to your room. *(ROY hands CECIL his doggy bag and the Armagnac. Then he puts his arm around him as they slowly head towards CECIL'S room)*

LIGHTS FADE

BLACKOUT
CURTAIN